Tom looked at the envelope in Lucy's hand and quickly stepped back against the horse. The fear in his eyes was chilling. Lucy just stood with her arm outstretched, feeling foolish, until Tom snatched the envelope abruptly. "Okay," he muttered, and slumped back against Moonrock, his eyes now as blank as the rest of his face.

"See you," Lucy said weakly, and walked slowly down the aisle. Suddenly, over the sounds of moving horses and rustling hay, she heard a rhythmic pounding. She followed the noise back to Moonrock's stall. Tom had no idea she was there. With all his strength he was driving his fist again and again into wooden board of the stall. Lucy caught her breath. Blood trickled from his knuckles. As she walked back to the annex door the pounding of her heart seemed as loud as the sound behind her.

CLAIRE BIRCH has written and produced many well-known documentaries on a variety of subjects. She lives in New York City.

ALSO AVAILABLE IN LAUREL-LEAF BOOKS:

A Lucy Hill Mystery #1

TIGHT SPOT

Claire Birch

LAUREL-LEAF BOOKS bring together under a single imprint outstanding works of fiction and nonfiction particularly suitable for young adult readers, both in and out of the classroom. Charles F. Reasoner, Professor Emeritus of Children's Literature and Reading, New York University, is consultant to this series.

Published by
Dell Publishing Co., Inc.
1 Dag Hammarskjold Plaza
New York, New York 10017

Laurel-Leaf Library ® TM 766734, Dell Publishing Co., Inc.

ISBN: 0-440-98732-6

RL: 4.7 reading level

Printed in the United States of America

First Printing—April 1985

To Phebe Jensen and William Wise,
who helped put Lucy in the saddle.

Chapter One

Lucy Hill felt the same lift of excitement every time the car reached the sign at the stable drive. She read the words UP AND DOWN FARM, above the picture of the horse's head, as if returning a greeting.

Mrs. Hill drove their Toyota up the private dirt road and Lucy checked the scene. The Beginners' Ring was empty. In the Main Ring across the way one of the older girls was moving a rangy chestnut down a line of fences. The red-and-white jump rails scattered color across the background of green fields.

"Mom, look at Liz on her new jumper. That horse is jet-propelled!"

Mrs. Hill glanced at the ring quickly, then turned back to the road. She held the steering wheel so tightly, a tiny white patch showed at the tip of each knuckle.

As they drove past the paddock toward the cluster of buildings up ahead, Mrs. Hill said, "You're supposed to come home with Debby Sherman today, remember?"

"Yeah."

"*Yes,* Lucy. The word is *yes.*"

"Of course I remember. You and Dad have that appointment." It seemed so strange that her parents, of all people, should be going to a marriage counselor. But maybe a counselor could help them stop arguing. Lately, her mother and father always seemed angry at each other.

Mrs. Hill followed the road to the right and pulled up in front of the old yellow farmhouse that held the stable office. The brakes had barely gripped when Lucy jumped from the car. "See you at home," she called over her shoulder.

But her mother's unhappiness hung in the air behind her. By now the Toyota was backing into a turn between the barn and the Indoor Ring. Mrs. Hill's slim body twisted at the wheel and her short brown hair swung to one side. Lucy tugged at her own brown hair; now that she'd reached fifteen, it had finally grown a few inches past her shoulders.

"Did you forget something?" Mrs. Hill called out.

"No, Mom." Lucy walked to the car and aimed a kiss at her mother's cheek. Though it landed in the air, she felt better. Turning away, she deliberately closed everything out of her mind but the world of Up and Down Farm. The office door whined shut behind her.

Sally Lomax, the twenty-year-old who helped in the office, peered at Lucy through steel-rimmed glasses from behind a huge oak desk. The desk had been made over a hundred years ago for the first Kendrick to own Up and Down Farm.

"Hello, Lucy. Did you see Mr. Kendrick out there?"

"No. Was I supposed to?"

"He took Moonrock out on the trail. I wondered if he was back."

Lucy knew that she and Sally were thinking the same thing. Mrs. Kendrick had died about a year and a half ago. For a while Mr. Kendrick had taken to riding off on Moonrock, his big brown hunter, at odd times of the day. But this afternoon was the first time he'd done that in many months.

"I'm supposed to work with him at four o'clock."

"Right. He said he'd be back." Sally rolled an envelope into the typewriter.

"Is something the matter?" Lucy said.

"Not especially."

"Come on, Sally. Mr. Kendrick's out on the trail. You're chewing your lip."

"I don't know what's bothering Mr. K.," Sally said. *"My* problem's the June first board bills."

"What's the big deal? You do them every month."

"I don't like crossing out the riders we've lost."

"Has anyone else gone?" Lucy asked anxiously.

"Judy Miller's leaving tomorrow. That makes the fifth Junior rider to take off."

"For Wilmont Farms, of course?"

"Of course."

"I wish I had a driver's license. I'd go take a look at that new stable."

"You're not going to leave us, too, are you?" Sally laughed and typed out another envelope.

"Very funny. But I would like to look at that place and those Hodgsons who run it. They're beginning to get in our hair." She glanced at the wall clock behind the desk. "I'd better go for Peanuts."

"Not old Peanut Butter today." Sally hitched her

chair closer to the desk. "You're riding Silver Whistle."

"Mrs. Kelly's horse? Me? Come on, Sally."

"I just repeat what I'm told. The Indoor Ring at four o'clock. Tom will have the mare ready."

Trying to conceal her excitement, Lucy started for the door. In half an hour she would have her first chance ever to ride a truly great horse. Hunters like Whistle cost thousands and thousands of dollars and not just anyone was allowed to ride them.

"You'll love Whistle," Sally added. "She's got gorgeous gaits. And she makes four-foot fences seem like toothpicks."

"You can bet you'll hear all about it!"

Lucy stepped out of the office into the clear spring air. Taking a deep breath, she surveyed the Connecticut countryside. In the last few years a group of development houses had sprouted in the fields across the Main Road. But on either side of Up and Down Farm stretches of open land extended the beautiful view. A horse whinnied in the paddock, and from the Beginners' Ring children's voices pierced the country calm. School would be out in a few more weeks and she could spend most of each day at the stable. Another summer of intensive riding would begin. And today, a lesson on Whistle! What a warm-up.

"Well, hello there, Lucy. I don't often see you standing around daydreaming."

Nick Walker, the elderly stable carpenter, had a head of white hair, but his back was straight and his muscles bulged as he carried a tall stepladder toward the barn.

"Hi, Nick. What are you fixing today?"

"Same roof I've been patching on and off for years."

Nick opened up his ladder and looked across the north field toward the entrance to the wooded trails. "Here comes young John now," he said.

Lucy laughed to herself. "Young John" was Mr. Kendrick—some name for a man in his fifties. But Nick had worked for old Mr. Kendrick when "young John" was just a kid.

As Mr. Kendrick cantered toward them, Lucy realized she'd never really thought of him as young or old. His red hair was turning a creamy white and thinning out over the top of his head. There were deep wrinkles around his pale blue eyes and along the sides of his mouth. But everything about him seemed powerful and sure. She watched him move along on Moonrock as though he were meant to be in the saddle and no place else.

"Hello, Lucinda," he called, reining in at the edge of the parking area. "I'll be ready for you in about five minutes."

"Sure, Mr. Kendrick. And . . . *thanks.* About Whistle, I mean."

"We'll see how you make out with her," Mr. Kendrick said with a thin, wide smile.

He called to Nick and walked on toward the barn. Nick waved and started up the twelve-foot stepladder easily. Almost at the top rung, the old man began to wobble. Lucy froze as the ladder pitched sideways, taking Nick with it.

"Lucy!" Mr. Kendrick shouted, vaulting from his horse. Lucy raced to take Moonrock's reins, but her eyes were riveted to the ground. Nick lay under an end of the ladder, so very still he might even have stopped breathing.

"I'm really beat," Lucy said half an hour later as she and her best friend, Debby Sherman, sat on the grass near the paddock.

"I'm glad I didn't see Nick out cold," Debbie said. "He was beginning to come around when I got here." Her short black curls shone in the sunlight and her dark eyes were large circles in a soft round face. She pulled a chocolate bar from her pocket. "Want a piece of candy?"

Lucy shook her head. "Poor Nick," she said. "He looked so pale when the ambulance guys carried him off on the stretcher. He must have broken some bones, for sure."

"Would you like to go home, Lucy? We can leave earlier, if you want to."

"No, thanks. I can work with Peanuts even if Mr. Kendrick isn't here. Besides, I don't want to be home when my folks get back from their big talk."

"Are things any better between them?"

"Who knows? None of it makes sense to me."

Debby looked closely at Lucy. "You know, you're a perfect cross between your parents."

"I hear that all the time."

"You've got your mother's brown hair and her perfect features . . . your face is long like your father's—"

"Yeah, and my green eyes are a mixture of both. You know, Debby, sometimes now that they're not getting along, I feel as though I'm being pulled apart myself."

Lucy opened a button at the top of her shirt. After

months of down vests and flannel the freedom of one
layer of cotton felt great.

"I knew Mr. Kendrick would go off in the ambulance with Nick," she said. "He was terrific. He kept
his cool when a man he's loved since he was a little
boy seemed to be lying there dead."

"Honestly, Lucy. Mr. Kendrick's all grown up now.
What's so wonderful about calling the volunteer am-
bulance without losing your head? You always make
Mr. Kendrick ten feet tall."

Lucy sat up straight and pulled at the laces of a
paddock boot.

"It's true," Debby said. "Mr. Kendrick is great, but
for you he's unreal. I've never understood it."

"Well, no one has ever helped me more . . . or
made me feel better about myself."

"I know he lets you teach the beginners in ex-
change for extra lessons, and he's found you horses
to work with—"

"It's more than the riding."

"There's a reason I haven't heard?"

"Well, yeah." Lucy tightened the laces on the second boot. "You've met my brother, Eric. He's a tough
act to follow. He's friendly, gorgeous, brilliant . . . especially brilliant. And my mother has this lopsided
worship of brains."

"You mean she's played favorites?"

"Not exactly. I know she loves me. But Eric is her
kind of special. And compared to him I have nothing
going in the brain department."

"So-o, Kendrick let you know you were his kind of
special."

"Yeah—I mean yes. Mr. Kendrick taught me to

measure against myself and no one else. He made me get to know Lucy Hill."

"Seems to me I've heard that tape."

"Okay, so he has some tapes he plays over and over, but this one worked for me."

Debby sat quietly. "Look, Lucy," she said after a while. "I can see why you and Kendrick are special friends. But even friends should see each other clearly."

"What don't I see?"

"That Mr. Kendrick isn't perfect. Remember Mr. Burke's horse and the medication?"

"Oh, that."

"Mr. Kendrick was supposed to give the horse the medication when he made his last round of the barn at eleven o'clock. He didn't do it."

"The horse is okay, isn't he?"

"*Now,* yes, but not then. He was sick for weeks because he wasn't started on the antibiotic."

"How do you know? Maybe Mr. Kendrick gave him the medicine and it wasn't strong enough."

"Don't you remember? Mr. Kendrick *told* Mr. Burke that he'd been at fault. He didn't even give him an excuse."

"Mr. Kendrick doesn't believe in excuses," Lucy muttered. She looked off into space. "Even if that's all true, it was soon after Mrs. Kendrick died and he was very upset. Nothing like that could happen now."

"Maybe not. But I think Nick's accident was also Mr. Kendrick's fault in a way. Nick's over seventy. That's old to be climbing up and down tall ladders."

"You know what you sound like, Debby? As though

you're ready to leave for Wilmont stable and the Hodgsons. Debby Sherman, junior defector number six!"

Debby turned to look Lucy straight in the eye. "Listen, Lucy. Just because I admit Mr. Kendrick's human doesn't mean I don't respect him. He's great with kids and horses both. I'm not going to the Hodgsons unless I'm forced to."

"Debby! What does *that* mean?"

"My father was over here last week and had some kind of a run-in with Tom."

"Tom Roberts, the groom? How did your father get him to talk? Tom's said about three words in the three months he's been here."

"The thing is," Debby said, "that my father's a big corporate type. He's used to 'yes, sir' and 'no, sir' at the office. He certainly expects it from a kid who works around a stable."

"Tom's strange, but he's better with horses than anyone we've had around here in a long time. And he sleeps at the stable. That's important with so much vandalism going on."

"Don't worry," Debby said. "It's not a big deal yet, and anyway, I'd put up a fight."

Lucy whistled with relief. "Even if we weren't friends, the barn needs you and your horse to help us cream the Hodgsons this summer. They make such a fuss about 'showing,' the kids begin to believe they'll pick up all the ribbons on the East Coast. Well, you can bring home ribbons with Mr. Kendrick too. He just doesn't think chasing ribbons is the main point to riding."

"Look, Lucy, you want to ride in the Maclay class

at Madison Square Garden more than anything. You don't get there without chasing ribbons. Shall I remind you?" Debby teased. "Three Maclay classes at local shows just to get to the regional eliminations."

"It's written on my brain with Magic Marker."

"I've never understood why the Maclay is so darn important to you."

How could she explain? It was just something she had to do. "I want to be the best rider I can be. The Maclay is the top of the hill for hunt seat riders under eighteen."

Lucy stood up and brushed the loose grass off her jeans. "I'd better get Peanuts." With only three years to go, she thought, I have to make every minute count.

Lucy put Peanuts through the usual warm-up routine in the Main Ring, then worked on the flat in both directions. She realized, though, that her concentration was off. She'd tried to put aside her disappointment over Whistle, ashamed to be thinking of herself when Nick was hurt. But would there ever be another chance to ride the mare? How much easier a horse like that would make getting to the Garden!

Lucy caught herself quickly. She might never even have a horse of her own, let alone one like Whistle. If she got to be a good enough rider, there was at least the hope that someone would lend her a horse to show. But she was going to make it to the Garden some way, even if it had to be on Peanuts.

"Let's go for it, friend." Lucy leaned over and patted the stocky little chestnut. They worked hard over the jumps in the Main Ring, then headed for the outside course. Here the fences were farther apart to test a hunter's "way of going" in the field. Horses classed as "jumpers" were allowed to get over fences any way they could. "Hunters" were supposed to have good manners, to be safe and comfortable for chasing a fox cross-country.

As Lucy moved smoothly around the arc of fences that rimmed the field, Peanuts suddenly planted his feet and swerved to one side. Lucy looked down at a tiny puppy with a small girl running behind it. They must have darted out of the trees. A shiver ran down Lucy's back as she realized how close the child had come to being trampled.

The little girl scooped up the puppy and stared at Lucy with widening eyes.

"My horse won't hurt you," Lucy said gently, as she jumped off Peanuts. "Your puppy scared him. That's why he put on the brakes so fast." She knelt to the child's level. "I'm Lucy Hill. What's your name?"

"Gail." The voice was a whisper. "Gail Conroy."

"You must live near here."

The little girl pointed across the road to one of the new houses. She looked up at Peanuts and edged closer to Lucy.

"I like horses. I'm getting lessons when I'm eight."

"Great. Then I'll be your teacher. I teach most of the beginners here." Lucy stood up and offered her hand. "Let's walk up to the barn. I'll show you some of the other horses."

Gail looked at Lucy uneasily. "I'm not allowed to take lessons here."

"You're not allowed! What do you mean?"

Gail clasped the wriggling puppy and said nothing.

Finally, she spoke up. "Mommy says it's not careful here."

"That's not true!" Lucy said. "Mr. Kendrick is the most careful teacher there is."

The child stared back stolidly. "People told it to my Mommy. I heard them at Detino's." With the puppy yipping against her shirt, she turned and ran across the field.

Lucy's eyes felt hot. How many times had she started to ride without a hard hat only to be told firmly, "Not at this barn." How often had she begged to raise the jump rails only to hear, "We'll tighten up that seat some more first. I'm teaching you to ride, not to fly."

Detino's? The DeMartinos owned the family grocery store in the village. They'd known Mr. Kendrick for years and surely would have straightened out any silly talk they heard.

Too preoccupied to get back on her horse, Lucy brought the stirrup irons up against the saddle without thinking. Then she remembered how carefully Mr. Kendrick had explained the safety code years ago. "If the horse comes in with stirrups flapping, we know to look for the rider. If the irons are up, the rider's likely safe and the horse just got loose."

Lucy led Peanuts back to the barn. Surely this talk couldn't have anything to do with that incident of Mr. Burke's horse over a year ago. Was someone starting up rumors on purpose?

Near the Indoor Ring, Domino, one of the Dalmatians, chased the new black kitten who was not much bigger than the dog's own spots. In front of the office parents were picking up young riders. Liz was sitting

in her van while several of the kids from her Begin-
ner Jumpers class hung on the door, unwilling to let
her go. Debby was probably parked in the office
doing her homework. Sally was headed for the barn
to kiss her ugly little horse, Misfit, good-night as
usual.

Lucy thought how Mr. Kendrick had given all the
stable kids an extra family, one which often made the
problems of their own families easier. And now it was
all being threatened by Wilmont, and rumors that
were absolute lies.

What kind of people were the Hodgsons anyway?
Lucy thought of the dozens of stories her father had
told about the competition in his business—making
television commercials. People lied and pulled lots
of dirty tricks to steal accounts from each other.
Could the Hodgsons be spreading lies about Mr. Kendrick to take business away from Up and Down
Farm?

Chapter Two

A week later Lucy led her beginners' class from the barn to the ring. "I'll fall off if we canter today," Virginia was saying in a trembling voice.

"Nobody's going to canter today," Lucy said firmly. "By the time we canter you'll all be ready."

The youngest riders at Up and Down Farm learned to relax around horses by walking them to the Beginners' Ring on foot. But each child could draft an older person to walk with them. Liz was in the lineup today, along with Tom, the silent groom, and Jim Martin, the new carpenter. Nick was getting better, but now he would definitely retire.

Eight-year-old Carol walked next to Lucy with Superman. "He's coming too close," she wailed. "He's never been this close." The child's eyes became slits to shut out the large animal.

Lucy thought of her own trips to the Beginners' Ring with Superman just before her tenth birthday. She could still summon the feeling of walking on a slant, one hand pressed against the horse's shoulder to keep his hooves off her feet.

As they moved down the field, Lucy was surprised to hear shouts and laughter coming from the Main

Ring. Soon she could see six or seven teen-aged boys grouped along the rail. Inside the ring Scot and Steve Bolton—identical sixteen-year-old twins—were lined up side by side on their new matched bays.

The children filed into the Beginners' Ring and Lucy helped Carol into the saddle while Liz adjusted Paul's stirrups nearby.

"What do you think is going on over there?" Lucy said to Liz.

As if on signal the boys took off and raced up the ring over two lines of matched jumps.

"I don't like the look of it," Liz said. "Those kids don't deserve such beautiful horses anyway. They've never really worked hard at riding and they're not particularly talented, either."

"Well, you know Mr. Bolton. He likes to show off his money. Everything he buys has to cost a mint."

They watched the two blond heads bob up and down in the Main Ring as the twins cleared the fences. Lucy had always thought Steve was kind of cute even though he was pretty stuck on himself. Scot was too tough and never listened to anyone else but himself.

"Loo-cee, what's happening over there?" Paul said.

"Let's just pay attention to what we're doing, okay?" That goes for you too, Lucy told herself. "All right, gang. Out into a circle."

Over in the Main Ring a burst of cheers greeted the end of the race and the boys trotted over to their friends at the rail.

Lucy turned back to Liz. "After all his trouble finding a perfect pair, Mr. Kendrick would love to see those horses being used for 'cowboys and Indians.' "

"They know he's in the Indoor Ring with the intermediates," Liz said, "so they're safe."

"Are you going to tell Mr. Kendrick?"

"I'm not sure. He may have given them permission to come down here and pop a few fences. They're just showing off for their friends and the jumps are low." Liz shrugged. "I've got a lot of work to do." She started for the barn.

Jim followed, tall and thin in his striped carpenter's overalls. "I'll be nearby if anyone needs to be hammered together."

Lucy began her usual chant to the children circling on the dirt track: "Let your body relax at a walk. Paul, I didn't say slouch. Just relax with the motion of the horse."

To Lucy's surprise Tom lit a cigarette and stayed at the rail. Back at the barn Virginia had taken his hand without a word and he'd walked along with her down to the ring. Now she called, "Watch me, Tom. You promised. Stay until we trot."

But Tom wasn't watching Virginia. Lucy followed his eyes to the Main Ring. Some of the guys had climbed the rail and were running around the ring raising fences.

Lucy forced her mind back to her class. "All right, everybody. Shorten your reins and get ready to trot. Pretend you're trooping the colors for Prince Charles and Diana. Sit tall, legs tight . . . and . . . tr-ot."

The children started to post against a background of shouts from across the drive. Once again Scot and Steve dashed over a line of matched fences. Before long there was a round of shouts: "Higher. Move them up. Come on, higher."

Tom ground out his cigarette and started for the Main Ring. Lucy was astonished. Would silent Tom really have the courage to speak up and stop the kids from taking reckless chances with the horses? But he reversed his direction abruptly and walked toward the barn.

Get your head back here, Lucy scolded herself. Mr. Kendrick trusts you with these kids. She managed to concentrate on her lesson reasonably well, but she couldn't ignore the noise as the Boltons raised the jumps still again and another race took place. Then Scot marched his horse through the ring gate with his fist in the air, apparently the victor. Surrounded by laughing friends he rode Dylan up the stable drive. Steve came behind him on Bowie.

"Loo-cee, is Up and Down Farm named because of us, the 'up and downs'?"

"You're no 'up and down.' You're a limp sack of flour. Now post, Paul, *post.*"

The lesson was back on the track but Lucy had to admit she'd rather have followed the twins. They were so keyed up, she wondered what they'd be up to next.

When Lucy finally herded her beginners back to the barn, she could hear the boys' voices from the rear aisle where Dylan and Bowie were stabled. But by the time she'd helped everyone put their horses away—brushing coats and picking stones out of hooves—the sounds had died away. At last Lucy made her first trip to the tack room with a pair of saddles.

"Ah-h, Mr. Kendrick," Scot Bolton was saying, "you don't really mean that, do you?"

"You can be sure I mean it. You're lucky I even talk to you when you've been this far out of line." Mr. Kendrick sounded furious.

As Lucy stepped closer, she smelled cigarette smoke. Had those dumb guys actually lit up in the barn? That was the worst possible crime around a stable.

"Now, have I made myself clear?" Mr. Kendrick said. "Eastchester is *out*. You're not going to represent this barn until you understand what you've done. You've risked the lives of twenty-one horses just to play at being grown-up with your friends. And don't bring your friends around here again, either. You can't even be responsible for your own behavior. That's it. Now get going."

Mumbled responses mixed with the shuffling of feet moving toward the door. Lucy backed out of sight and waited for the boys to leave the barn before she went into the tack room. She'd recognized a few of the kids from school. They were part of the group that were supposed to be making trouble around town—whacking over mailboxes and wrecking the greens on the golf course with their motorbikes.

Mr. Kendrick was leaning against the saddle rack, lost in thought. The tiny muscle on the side of his cheek was moving back and forth. Lucy knew he must be disappointed as well as angry. The twins had been around the barn as long as she had.

"Well, hello there, Lucy." Mr. Kendrick said, straightening up and squaring his shoulders. "Let's try to turn this afternoon around. How about that lesson on Whistle?"

"You bet! Can I get her?"

"No, tell Tom. He handles her all the time. I'm going up to the house to smoke my pipe for a bit. I'll be waiting in the Indoor Ring when you get there."

Lucy was too excited to answer. She nodded quickly and hurried back into the barn. Tom was coming up the aisle with his strange loping stride.

"Hi, Tom. Mr. Kendrick wants you to get Silver Whistle ready. I'm supposed to have a lesson on her as soon as we can make it."

Without answering the boy turned back down the aisle and disappeared around the corner. Lucy stared after him. He was irritating, all right! After three months at the stable you'd think he could loosen up and say a few words.

She shrugged and went for her chaps and hard hat. When she returned Tom was leading Mrs. Kelly's gray mare to the cross ties.

"She's beautiful!" Lucy hurried toward them, admiring the elegant head and perfect proportions of the fine-boned horse.

Silently, Tom fastened a clip to each side of Whistle's halter. Lucy looked at his arms. There was almost no flesh between the bones and the skin. Suddenly, Tom seemed more pitiful than sullen. Lucy said the first thing that came into her head.

"Don't you think Silver Whistle is a perfect name for her?"

It was impossible to tell if Tom nodded or if it was just that his head moved up and down as he groomed the horse. She ached to get her hands on Whistle and begin to make friends. "Tom, can I help?" There was no sound but the brush passing over the mare's flank.

Okay. She'd just wait it out. Folding her arms across her chest, Lucy stepped back against the wall. Tom ignored her completely. From time to time he murmured to Whistle to move to one side or to pick up her foot. Lucy glared.

At last Tom went for the mare's tack and Lucy had the lovely horse to herself. She rubbed Whistle's chest and stroked her muzzle. Whistle blew an enormous clumsy kiss into Lucy's neck. They were immediately the best of friends.

Ten minutes later Lucy led Whistle into the Indoor Ring, a large rectangular arena with a dirt floor and a high curved roof. She was nervous about doing well on such a finely tuned horse, but as always, her confidence returned when she saw Mr. Kendrick.

"There you are, Lucinda," he said. He cupped his hands and gave Lucy a leg up.

Lucy gathered up the reins and urged Whistle out to the wall. She knew better than to ask the reason for this special ride. Mr. Kendrick would tell her when he wanted her to know. What she was supposed to do now was *concentrate*—Mr. Kendrick's most frequently used word.

"How does she feel to you?" Mr. Kendrick asked after several minutes.

"Great."

"Are you working up there? Are you finding the buttons to push?"

"I think so."

Lucy asked Whistle to stop and start. She moved her back and forth from a walk to a trot, learning the signals that would make the mare respond. For a horse as sensitive as this one, hand and leg signals had to be just right—strong enough to communicate, soft enough so they weren't resented.

"Trot a figure eight and show me what you've learned."

Even after the first loop Lucy knew she was trying too hard. "That's a doodle, not a school figure," Mr. Kendrick scolded, but Lucy kept at it until he was smiling.

At last, after another ten minutes on the flat, Mr. Kendrick adjusted a few jumps at the end of the ring. "All right," he said. Let's try her over some fences." Don't rush. Just nice and easy."

Lucy had begun to canter a slow circle when a shrill voice cut across the ring.

"John. John Kendrick!" Mrs. Raymond was standing at the ring entrance with her brown horse, Rebel.

Mr. Kendrick said quickly, "Hold it, Lucy." Let me see what this is about."

"Rebel almost broke his leg, John," Mrs. Raymond shouted. "The bridge over the creek gave way. Do you hear me? I'm furious, John."

As Mr. Kendrick strode down the ring, Lucy trotted along behind him. How could the bridge be broken? The trails were on Mr. Kendrick's property and Nick had checked them all the time. At least half the boards had been replaced a month ago. And Mr. Kendrick had been out there just last week.

"Walk him a short way for me, Nancy," Mr. Kendrick said. The horse was definitely limping, although not very badly.

"Let's have a look," Mr. Kendrick bent over and ran his hands down Rebel's hind leg.

"It's the bridge that needs looking to, John. Then we wouldn't be concerned with this at all. It was Nick's job to check the bridge. He was getting too old for his work and you know it."

Mr. Kendrick straightened up. "I'm sorry about this, Nancy. But I think it's a slight sprain, at worst. We'll see what Dr. Harris has to say." He turned to Lucy. "Take Whistle back to Tom. I'll catch up with you later."

Lucy left the ring frowning. If Rebel had broken a leg, the talk about carelessness would have spread like crabgrass. It was going to be bad enough anyway. Mrs. Raymond had planned to show the horse at Eastchester. Now that seemed unlikely, and she'd let the world know why.

Lucy jumped off Whistle and slowly began to raise the stirrups. A sound board just didn't break through. Could Nick have missed a plank that was rotting inside? Could someone possibly have sabotaged the bridge? Maybe the accident was related to the rumors in some way—part of a larger plan to hurt Mr. Kendrick's reputation.

Lucy brought Whistle to Tom and hurried across the north field. The afternoon sun laid pools of light on the trail as she walked along quickly, pleased that no riders had passed to question why she was out there on foot. At the sound of the brook she broke into a jog. It would be exciting to find some clue that would help Mr. Kendrick.

The broken plank was about halfway across the bridge, hanging in two pieces like a ruptured V. It was one of the new boards Nick had recently put in place. Through the splintered edges Lucy could see the rushing water, high with the late spring rains. She knelt and studied the break for saw marks. She rapped along both pieces of the board to see if they were solid. Nothing about the break seemed suspicious. There was no reason why it should have happened at all!

Lucy took off her paddock boots. Then she held on to the rocks supporting the end of the bridge and clambered down the bank. The cold water was to the top of her knees as she waded into the stream. At the damaged board she cocked her head to check the break from underneath.

It was dark under the low bridge and her position was awkward, but the raw wood at the edge of the break seemed to be two different colors—yellow at the top, brown toward the bottom. The yellow was the usual color of fresh wood. The brown seemed to be some kind of rot.

Had someone replaced a sound, new board with one that had dry rot at the center? Wasn't it more likely that Nick had been careless in choosing the board at the lumberyard? Rebel had been the unlucky horse to come along when the board was ready to go. But then, he'd been lucky too. It was his back leg that hit and not the the front. Otherwise there would have been a break for sure.

Lucy climbed up onto the bridge, filled with disappointment. This little expedition in defense of Mr. Kendrick had been a flop. If anything, the evidence fell on the wrong side.

*　　　*　　　*

This day has been one big pain, Lucy thought as she waited for her mother in the parking area: her ride on Whistle cut short before jumping *one* fence, her attempt at sleuthing a total bust.

Liz Meredith walked toward her from the barn. Lucy stared at the tall long-legged blond. Liz had the perfect build for a rider. And she was as kind and capable as she was beautiful. No wonder everyone adored her!

"Some strange guy's been holed up with Kendrick for almost half an hour," Liz said impatiently.

"That's odd. Especially at this hour."

"And how! If you see Mr. Kendrick, tell him I need to check some classes with him, okay? Sally wants the final entries for Eastchester on her desk by six o'clock. I've got a load of tack to clean."

As Liz walked off, Lucy looked toward the apartment at the back of the yellow house that Mr. Kendrick used in the daytime. Was he having trouble with Mrs. Raymond or her husband? Was anything else the matter?

I've got to cool it, Lucy thought. Since the problems between Mom and Dad took me by surprise, I'm always imagining the worst. I built a rumor campaign on what one little girl had to say. I turned a simple accident on the bridge into a conspiracy.

There was still no sign of a car on the stable road, only Tom bringing Moonrock back from the paddock for the night. The big brown horse nuzzled the boy's shoulder as they walked. They passed close by and Tom spoke to Lucy softly. She turned and stared after him. Had he actually said, "So long"?

Just then a bald, heavyset man left Mr. Kendrick's

apartment. Smiling broadly, he headed toward an
unfamiliar blue Cutlass parked behind the Indoor
Ring. As he walked past Lucy she saw that the smile
looked pasted between his cheeks; it wasn't a real
smile at all.

Chapter Three

When Lucy arrived at the stable on the afternoon before the Eastchester show, the Boltons' Mercedes station wagon was parked at the barn door with a deluxe horse trailer behind it. The twins were struggling to get Bowie up the ramp while Liz waited nearby with Dylan.

". . . So, you wanted to shake up my boys . . . scare them a little," Mr. Bolton was bellowing. "But I didn't think you'd be foolish enough to stick to what you said. Eastchester's their first show. I spent a fortune on those horses. You spent a lot of time on them. I thought we were after the same thing, Kendrick."

"What was that, Ralph?" Mr. Kendrick said slowly.

"Blue ribbons, that's what." He paused, "Look—I think you're way off base on the Town Council. You *know* that. I don't expect you to have smart ideas about zoning or real estate. But the stable is different."

Mr. Kendrick opened his mouth to answer, then closed it quickly. He drew a hand along his jaw.

"You know, Ralph, you're right," he said finally. "We're not after the same thing. I think it's a good idea to move your horses. Let's see if we can get this show on the road."

Lucy knew she should go into the barn to braid Peanuts's mane and tail for the show. But she wasn't about to miss the end of this scene.

"Take Dylan around in a circle, Scot," Mr. Kendrick said. "Then lead him straight up the ramp with Steve right behind him."

"What's wrong with you guys?" Bolton shouted. "All the time you've spent over here, you can't get a horse up a five-foot ramp? Get a move on."

"Maybe we should let Dylan calm down," Steve said. "Let's try Bowie first, okay?"

Steve took Bowie's lead shank from Liz and loaded him into the van without trouble. Scot moved quickly, and Dylan decided to follow.

Bolton scowled, "Now I suppose I'll have to wait another half hour for that dumb kid to have DiMaggio ready."

As if on cue Mr. Kendrick stepped aside and Tom walked out of the barn. Behind him DiMaggio, Mr. Bolton's beautiful black horse, was ready for travel—legs and tail neatly bandaged, a lightweight sheet in place.

"Let Tom put him in the van," Mr. Kendrick said. "He does very well with the horse."

Tom caught Mr. Kendrick's nod and kept on moving. The horse clattered up the ramp behind him. He secured the horse, ducked his head against his chest, and hurried back into the barn. The twins slammed the trailer door.

"I don't forget things like this, Kendrick. No one punishes my boys but me. If they need to be pulled up short, *I'll* do it." Bolton walked to the front of the station wagon and slid in behind the wheel. The boys joined him in the front seat and they drove away.

Lucy watched the car turn at the stable sign. It was sad to see DiMaggio leaving the stable. When she was small she'd looked for chances to feel his shiny coat; he glistened like a seal coming out of water.

All at once Mr. Kendrick let out his breath as if he'd been holding it a long time. "That man's left a bad taste in my mouth," he said, more to himself than to Lucy. He took a pipe from his pocket and, holding it unlit between his teeth, walked off toward the yellow house.

Lucy brought Peanuts into Debby's aisle so they could keep each other company braiding for the show. It still took Lucy fifty minutes for a mane and an hour for a tail, so going it alone was a bore.

Debby was in the aisle next to Redford, talking to Jim, the carpenter.

"I'll have it fixed by tomorrow, Debby," Jim said, examining the stall door where the hinge had pulled loose.

"Hi, Jim," Lucy said.

"Hello, Lucy. By the way," he said, very seriously. "There's something I've been meaning to ask you girls."

"Oh?" Lucy said.

"What's that?" Debby said.

"When is a horse not a horse?"

Lucy groaned. "Tell that to my beginners, but don't be surprised if they've heard it before."

Jim went right on. "When it's a *chestnut*. Bye, girls."

Debby watched him saunter down the aisle. "He's not too bright, but don't you think he's handsome?"

"I guess so," Lucy put Peanuts in the crossties. "He's got big brown eyes and a terrific cleft chin but it's all too obvious, like some kind of a shirt ad."

"Well, I think he's cool," Debby said. "Have you noticed how some of the mothers like to stand around and talk to him?"

Lucy shrugged and pulled over a tack trunk. She climbed up and began to separate the horse's mane into sections. "It won't do any good. He's hung up on that gorgeous Anita he goes with."

"Did you see his car?" Debby asked.

"Who could miss a bright blue T-bird? Sally told me Jim bought it because Anita wouldn't ride around in his old heap anymore."

Debby climbed back up on a chair next to Redford and braided a thick piece of thread into a section of his mane. "You're going to look so spiffy tomorrow," she crooned to her horse, "the judge won't be able to resist you."

"Debby, I've been meaning to ask you," Lucy said. "Why don't you ever show in equitation classes? You're a very good rider. You've got the neatest pair of hands—"

Debby reacted fast. "No, thanks. I'd rather they judge Redford than me."

Of course, Lucy thought. When Debby was showing Redford, she was confident and competitive. She was a fighter for her friends too. But she would never go after anything for herself. Not that anyone could push her around! She just wouldn't try to compete.

"Lucy, tomorrow's got to be a good day for you," Debby said eagerly. "You've *got* to win Limit over fences."

Equitation classes took place over fences and "on the flat." Riders advanced from Maiden, through Novice and Limit, to Open. Lucy had already won six blue ribbons in flat classes, but to graduate from Limit she needed two more over fences. Then she'd ride in Open classes with only the most advanced riders and begin to concentrate on the Maclay.

"You'd have made it to Open long ago, Lucy, if you'd had your own horse. Mr. Kendrick does his best to find something for you, but it's always temporary, and when you have to change horses in the middle of the summer . . ."

Lucy didn't need to be reminded. The problem was always the same. The private horses were seldom available and the school horses couldn't do her much good.

"How long did you ride, Debby, before you had your own horse? Was Redford the first?"

"Technically, yes. Dad bought him for me when we got back to the states. But when we were in Germany, I had the use of a wonderful Hanoverian. I called him 'Spaetzle' after those noodlelike things we ate all the time."

"You must have hated to leave him behind."

"I've had practice leaving things behind. You forget, we've lived in four different countries over the last ten years. By the way, my mother says she's coming to the show tomorrow."

"Hey!" Lucy said enthusiastically.

Quietly, Debby began to loop a braid against the horse's neck. Lucy thought she was probably wondering if her mother would actually show up. Was it worse to have parents who weren't getting along or parents who were never there?

"Things change," Debby said. "Take my family. After all that moving around Dad got his big job at corporate headquarters. Maybe they still travel a lot, but Westlake is home. Wait and see. I bet you'll have your own horse someday."

"Maybe," Lucy said.

"Things have certainly changed for Mr. Kendrick," Debby said as her fingers worked away. "For the first time there's a competing stable nearby—"

"And tomorrow we'll see 'the whites of their eyes.'"

"Look, Lucy. We're not going into battle. It's supposed to be fun."

Sometimes Lucy wished she could go along with life as easily as Debby. But she just wasn't made that way. When she wanted something, she wanted it hard. When she was worried about something, she couldn't get it out of her mind.

"You're right, Debby," Lucy said. "It's our first show of the year and I can hardly wait."

But to herself she said: At least in the show ring, the Hodgsons have to beat us fair and square.

Lucy turned over in bed and squinted at the tiny red numbers that glared in the dark. She cleared her head. It was four twenty-seven on Saturday, the morning of the Eastchester show. Though she was always afraid to take a chance, her inner alarm clock had worked again. There were still three minutes left to enjoy her warm bed and the stillness of the early morning. Her blue riding jacket hung on the closet door next to a wheat-colored shirt and a mono-grammed choker. The boots she'd brought to a high sheen the night before stood firm on the boot trees.

She rolled over, thinking out her classes. Okay, remember not to rush the last fence. Remember! Two numbers changed on the face of the clock. The alarm buzzed.

It was still dark outside when Lucy walked into the kitchen.

"Hi, Dad," she said, sliding into a chair at the round table in the corner.

"Good morning, Mite." Her father was the one who usually drove these early trips to the barn, and Lucy was pleased to see him up on time. He'd put a tumbler of orange juice in front of her place. He was sipping his own juice as if it were medicine.

"Thanks, Dad. Every minute counts."

"That's something I've never understood—why you get up so early even when the show's nearby. It seems like masochism to me. In fact, the whole riding venture seems like self-torture." The smile on Mr. Hill's face left no doubt that he was teasing. Lucy looked at his eyes, deep set in an angular face. She thought he looked haggard.

"It's not self-torture," she said. "Just hard work. We have to bandage the horses' legs and tails to get them ready to ship. Then there's travel time for the van, and 'schooling time'—practicing when we get there."

Mr. Hill toyed with his juice glass. He pushed his chair away from the table. "Can I make you a 'name' pancake?"

"Sure, Dad, great," Lucy said, though she never wanted much breakfast the morning of a show.

This routine went back as long as Lucy could remember. The thin pancake would be folded over raspberry jam and ceremoniously put on a plate. Then it would be dedicated to a special "name."

At the counter Mr. Hill seemed to be whipping the eggs much longer than usual.

"This is for Peanuts," Lucy said. "He's going to help me get another blue ribbon today."

Her father's mind was somewhere else. She could tell from the listless way he poured the yellow liquid into the frying pan.

"We've had some great times in this house, haven't we?"

Lucy looked up. What was coming next?

"I don't have to tell you that your mother and I haven't been getting along."

"No," she said carefully, "you certainly haven't been getting along *lately.*"

Mr. Hill put a lopsided pancake in front of Lucy. "You have to understand, Lucy. The 'lately' started long ago."

"I suppose so." Lucy cut the pancake into one tiny section after another. She wasn't going to get involved in this today if she could help it.

"Mom and I are still good friends. We'll always pull together for you and Eric, you know that."

"Sounds good," she said. "I really should leave in about ten minutes. Will that be okay?"

"Sure, Lucy. Sure."

Lucy slid off her chair and circled the table until she was standing behind her father. She put her arms around his shoulders and hugged him hard. He stood up and they left the kitchen together. Lucy's pancake lay uneaten on her plate.

As they drove along the winding roads to Up and Down Farm, Lucy tried to keep her mind off the breakfast conversation. Now, what were the three most important things Mr. Kendrick had said to remember? Number one: Don't rush the last fence. Without thinking, Lucy reached over and rested her hand on her father's knee. They drove along that way in silence as they had done when she was a little girl.

"See you, Dad." At the stable Lucy grabbed her coat and hurried to the barn. No one was in sight but Rudi, the driver, half asleep in the front seat of the large horse van. Some of the horses should have been loading by now.

The barn was strangely quiet. As she reached the far aisle, Lucy saw Sally parked on a tack trunk. Eddy Cooper, one of the older riders, who also worked as a groom, was pacing back and forth, his chin on his chest.

"What's going on?" Lucy asked cautiously.

"Someone's gone scissor happy," Eddy said.

"What are you talking about?"

"Look at the horses," Sally said.

In a nearby stall Tom ran his fingers through Orion's mane. The threads had been cut and the braids opened up. There were crimps all along the tangled hair.

"That's crazy. Are they all like that?"

"Twelve manes, twelve tails. And today of all days."

Lucy knew what Sally meant. The first time Up and Down Farm showed against the Hodgsons, the horses just *had* to look their best.

"Tom came downstairs about half an hour ago," Sally went on. "The locks on the barn were broken and the horses were like this."

"Is anything missing?" Lucy asked.

"Nothing we could see. Tom and I checked together." Sally chewed on her lip. "Mr. Kendrick's going to call any second to see how we're doing. I hate to tell him the bad news."

"It's weird, Sally. Doesn't it seem like spite?"

"That's what I think," Eddy said. "Two spoiled brats thumbing their noses at Mr. Kendrick."

"It wasn't just the usual vandals. They'd never have thought of this. It had to be someone who knew they were setting us back . . . like the twins . . . or"—Lucy bit her lip before she said, "the Hodgsons."

"Hello, guys, I thought you'd be all braided by now," Liz joked from the head of the aisle.

Eddy laughed. "We wouldn't start the party without you."

"Let's go." Sally slid off the tack trunk. "Tom's done the bandaging."

"Great." Liz said. "Why don't we work in pairs on the horses with the earliest classes? There's about twenty-five minutes before the van has to leave."

"I'll go in the van with Tom and we can braid on the way," Sally suggested.

"Me too," Lucy added.

"I got here as fast as I could, Sally." Jim hurried toward them, oddly unfamiliar in blue jeans and a snappy plaid shirt.

"Great!" Liz said. "Right now you can cut thread. I'll get you started."

"Jim, are you coming to the show?" Lucy asked.

"Can't today. I'm seeing Anita."

"Bring her too. We need a big cheering section."

"Sorry. We're driving to Boston in my new car. Next time, though."

Everyone pitched in and four horses were ready when Lucy left in the van along with Sally and Tom. No one talked as they rumbled along the Connecticut back roads, each braiding in separate compartments.

Alone with Peanuts, Lucy replayed the conversation with her father in her head. She knew she shouldn't think about it now and forced her mind back to the stable. This business of the braids was weird, all right, and the twins were certainly the most likely suspects. But she could think of other motives besides spite. How about unsettling Mr. Kendrick's riders on an important day? How about adding to the impression of confusion at the barn?

When Peanuts was ready, Lucy looked out of one of the small windows in the van. The gray light of early morning was lifting. It was going to be a perfect show day, sunny but not too warm. Pink paper signs on trees and telephone poles began to point the way. Up ahead a car pulled a horse trailer. Two girls trotted along the side of the road with red yarn braided into their horses' manes.

The van drove into the show grounds and parked in the paddock area. Lucy and Sally rushed to the show stand to collect their numbers.

Near the raised platform a cluster of people from Up and Down Farm surrounded Mr. Kendrick. Someone's mother was practically shouting. "She's not entered at all. Not in a single class!"

As Lucy and Sally joined the group, Debby was trying to be heard. "Mr. Kendrick, Mrs. Patton said she didn't receive *any* entries from Up and Down Farm. It's not just some of us. It's *all* of us."

"This is outrageous," one of the fathers exclaimed. It's not like you, Kendrick. Not like you at all."

Chapter Four

"Quiet, everybody, and listen carefully."

Mr. Kendrick pulled a folded piece of paper from inside his jacket and looked squarely from one person to another. "I've a list of your classes right here. Five minutes with Mrs. Patton, the show secretary, and we'll have post entries for everyone. Your class goes first, Jessica," he said to the stable's youngest rider. "Sally will help you get your horse and I'll bring your number to the schooling area. The rest of the numbers will be at the van."

Mr. Kendrick paused a moment as though reining in his temper. "We'll get to the bottom of this morning's problems, but not today. Concentrate. Do your best. The weather's beautiful. Let's have a good time."

As he stepped up on the wooden platform under the green-striped awning, Lucy and Debby moved closer. Mrs. Patton was working behind a table covered with class lists.

"John, I'm sorry about that flap with your group, but I haven't a trace of your entries."

"They were mailed two weeks ago, Peggy. We could have *walked* them here in an hour."

"You know how careful I am when I run a show. You'd better check at your end," Mrs. Patton said firmly. "Now, how do we set it right?"

Mr. Kendrick handed over his duplicate list and waited for Jessica's number. Then he turned to the girls.

"Debby, you get up to the van and make sure the horses we need in the morning are braided. Lucy, you wait for the numbers and take them to the van." He started to walk away, then stopped short. "Thanks, girls. I'll see you in the schooling area as usual—thirty minutes before each class."

What was wrong with this day anyway? Lucy wondered. Had she put her right boot on first instead of her left? That was always bad luck.

Lucy waited impatiently as Mrs. Patton recorded their entries class by class. Parents and children interrupted constantly, eager to claim their numbers. Some of the riders tied on the white paper squares then and there, walking off with bold black numerals on their backs.

A solemn-faced girl of about twelve pushed her way up to the table. Lucy tried not to stare at the hearing aid in her ear and the built-up boot on her foot.

"Dena Altschuler," the girl said. "Wilmont Farms."

As Dena limped away, Lucy looked after her, impressed that someone with her handicap had the spunk to ride in a horse show. The first Hodgson entry certainly wasn't the ideal riding material she'd expected.

"All right, Lucy," Mrs. Patton said at last. "I've put

the rider's name on the back of each number. Tell
John to stop by later and pay his entry fees. Otherwise I'll have to impound the trophies you're all
going to carry off today."

Lucy smiled back and grabbed the numbers. As
she started for the van, the loudspeaker crackled.
"Testing, one, two. Testing, one, two. Good morning
and welcome to the Eastchester Show. Will the riders for class fourteen, Maiden Horsemanship on the
flat, come to the ingate in fifteen minutes, please? We
will be ready for class fourteen at eight o'clock
sharp."

Lucy always felt excited at the first loudspeaker an-
nouncement of the day. Suddenly the morning's
problems seemed trivial and far away. The fun and
the challenge were about to begin.

By midmorning the paddock area was filling up
with vans and trailers. Lucy dodged horses all the
way as she hurried to the ingate with a rag for
Debby's boots.

"Hey, Lucy." Scot Bolton was trotting by on Dylan.
He brought the horse to a halt.

"Hello, Scot." Lucy's voice was guarded.

"We're showing today after all."

"So I see."

"Well, why not? We've got a right to be here."

Lucy said nothing.

"We were at Up and Down Farm this morning—"

"Really? I thought you might have been."

"It was real early. I left a cooler behind that we
needed today."

"Did anyone see you?"

"I heard Tom stomping around but I didn't stop to talk." Scot laughed. "Hey, I guess that's sort of funny, seeing he *never* talks. Anyway, I hear you had some trouble about the braids. Real crazy, huh?"

"How come *you* know about the braids, Scot? Hardly anyone knows."

"The guy who drives the van told me. See ya." Scot tightened his legs on Dylan and rode off. Lucy looked after him. Those guys were hard to figure.

A little later Lucy and Debby found a good spot at the rail for Liz's Green Jumper class.

"You see that tall, thin woman with the thick blond braid down her back?" Lucy nodded her head to one side. "I think that's Mrs. Hodgson."

"How do you know?"

"The girl beside her, number 36, rides at Wilmont Farms."

"Come on. Let's move over there."

Mrs. Hodgson was watching a tall boy in the ring who rode a horse that seemed too small for him. As he pounded past, she said quietly, "Good, Martin. Keep him moving." The horse breezed over the course until the "in and out." Here two fences, set close together, needed more stamina than the horse had left. The top rail of the second fence rolled to the ground.

"Oh, Mrs. Hodgson," Dena Altschuler said, as the woman beside her groaned softly.

"It was a beautiful ride all the same. Who is he?" Lucy whispered to Debby.

"I don't know, but he's gorgeous! *She* seems nice enough."

Lucy didn't answer. She gripped Debby's elbow as Liz trotted through the ingate. There was a bad moment when Shogun's hind leg rolled a rail forward, but it settled back into place. He'd gone "clean" at the fastest time so far. Lucy and Debby clapped loudly as Liz left the ring. No other horse matched her round. She'd brought the stable the first blue of the day.

By eleven thirty Lucy's stomach was rumbling. Debby had been talking about food for the last hour. Together they walked to the Shermans' oversized station wagon, parked at ringside. From the car they would be able to watch the show while they ate.

Bryan, the Shermans' chauffeur, smiled at them from behind the wheel. "Sometimes I think Bryan and Tina are more my parents than my mother and father," Debby said, opening the door to the back of the wagon. "I've known them almost as long, and I see more of them."

"But your mother's coming this afternoon, isn't she?"

"Don't bet on it. Bryan's been trying to break it to me gently all morning."

"I thought you'd get here about now." Bryan pointed to the picnic cooler that Tina, the Shermans' cook, had packed. "You did great, Debby. Don't be shy today. Let me hang the ribbon on the window." He reached for the yellow rosette Debby had won with Redford in her Junior Hunter class.

As Lucy enjoyed a thick roast-beef sandwich and one of Tina's special brownies, she began to relax.

"We've really pulled it off this morning, don't you think?"

"You bet. In spite of everything, we've all gone into the ring looking great, and we're winning too."

"I think we're about to pick up another blue for Pleasure Horse."

As Lucy watched the ring, a high-pitched voice intruded from a neighboring car. "Everyone says that Kendrick is slipping."

The girls looked at each other, then sat absolutely still.

"I wouldn't say that," a second woman's voice answered. "His entries are doing very well today."

"Maybe. But did you hear about the commotion this morning? The entry list never got to the show at all. Of course they blamed the mail. But what I'm hearing all over town is carelessness, lack of interest in the kids . . ."

"Not Kendrick. I don't believe it."

"Look, Nan Seymour's horse went through a neglected bridge. She couldn't show today."

Lucy swallowed a piece of sandwich so fast she almost choked. "Debby, there *must* be a rumor campaign! Remember the little kid I told you about who was chasing her dog—the one whose mother had heard Up and Down Farm wasn't safe? Now this woman has been hearing things 'all over town.' I feel like taking an ad in the *Westlaker:* 'Death to Rumormongers. Long live John Kendrick!' "

"Lucy Hill, terrorist." They both laughed.

"Hey, there are your parents." Debby pointed to the Hills' Toyota as it pulled into a space at ringside.

"I don't want to see them right now. I'm going up to the van." Lucy opened the station wagon door.

"Hey, wait. I'm right behind you."

Lucy's first class was the big one, Limit over fences, where she had her best chance for another blue ribbon. No one could ride in this class who'd won more than six blues. Her Open classes later in the day would mean tougher competition.

The first four fences felt good, but rounding the bottom of the ring for the second trip, she broke her concentration and glanced at the judge. Though she caught herself quickly, she had trouble setting up Peanuts for the fifth fence. The rest of the ride was fine, but Lucy knew she'd blown it—and with the kind of dumb mistake you make in your first show.

Mr. Kendrick was waiting at the outgate. "I don't need to tell you what happened."

"No."

"The rest of the ride was good." He patted Peanuts.

Lucy looked down at the horse's withers. "It won't happen again."

"Right."

As Mr. Kendrick walked away, Liz ran up to Lucy. "Don't look so glum. It wasn't that bad."

"Come on. Even when I rode in Maiden I knew better than to look at the judge."

Liz grinned. "So you're human, like the rest of us."

Lucy listened halfheartedly as the loudspeaker blared the results of the of the class. "First, number seventy-two, Anna Windecker. Second, number thirty-six, Dena Altschuler. . . ."

"That's the girl with the bad leg," Lucy said. "Good for her."

"Third, number forty-two, Lucy Hill."

"I told you it wasn't that bad!" Liz said. "Go get it."

Lucy trotted toward the ingate. She was glad to bring home another ribbon for the stable. But she was furious at herself just the same.

Lucy had taken Peanuts to the van and was on her way to see her parents when her mother walked toward her.

"There you are, Lucy. I brought you a Thermos of apple juice."

"Thanks, Mom. I can use some right now. Where's Dad?"

"In the car. We've been here over an hour. Why didn't you come to say hello?"

"It's been a tough day, Mom. I was braiding at the van most of the morning."

"I thought that was all done the day before."

"Usually. I mean it was." Lucy's stomach tightened. She wasn't going to add to the talk about the stable.

"Look, I'm sorry Mom. I have responsibilities at a show—for me and for the barn."

"Of course." Mrs. Hill poured some more juice into the plastic cup. "Roberta Donatello and I were just talking about how much responsibility you and Amy have developed through your riding. Evidently Amy's learned more than ever since she's been at the new stable."

"Well, isn't that just great. Amy was with Mr. Kendrick for three years. She's been at Wilmont Farms for three months. And her mother doesn't know the first thing about riding, anyway—"

"Calm down, Lucy. I'm glad you're loyal to Mr. Kendrick," Mrs. Hill said. "He's a fine teacher. How many more classes do you have?"

"Two. I'll be at least another hour and a half."

"Dad and I don't mind waiting. Look for us when you're through." Mrs. Hill gave Lucy's arm a squeeze.

As Lucy watched her mother walk off, she began to get angry. In the morning her father had made it sound as if they were all washed up. Now they were cozily sitting in the car, enjoying the show together. She wished they'd make up their minds.

Lucy stepped back suddenly as Liz, on Shogun, almost ran into her.

"Lucy, have you got a Kleenex to wipe my boots?"

Flustered, Lucy searched her pockets.

"Never mind. There's Joey Rose. Hey, Joey," Liz called, "come here a minute."

An eight-year-old with a face full of freckles ran toward her so fast the ice cream he was licking fell off the cone.

"Too bad, kid. Run up to the van, get a rag from Tom, and bring it to me. Then I'll give you a dollar for another cone."

"That's okay, Liz," Joey said eagerly, and raced off.

"If only he was twice as old and half again as tall," Liz said, laughing.

"Liz, Tom should be down here with a rag."

"Of course," Liz said, "but he hasn't been around the ring or the schooling area at all today."

"Well, in the morning he was braiding."

"Okay, but it's three o'clock in the afternoon. I'm surprised. Tom may not talk much, but he usually does what he's supposed to. Mr. Kendrick gave him instructions. I heard him."

"Let's go, Liz," Mr. Kendrick called. "Take Shogun over to the ingate."

Today's complications just don't seem to end, Lucy thought as she watched Liz ride off with Mr. Kendrick. Why on earth was Tom hanging around at the van?

A second place in Open "on the flat" helped Lucy feel better about the morning's goof. Placing against tougher competition meant that she was improving. Now Open "over fences" was coming up. She couldn't expect much there, but at least she'd remember not to look at the judge.

"Tom, it's me, Lucy," she called as she came to the van for her horse.

Tom poked his head in and out of the door like a turtle. Then he brought Peanut Butter down the ramp, tacked up and ready to go.

As Lucy took the horse, Mrs. Wilson, one of the adult riders, advanced toward them both. "You wouldn't know it, hidden away up here," she said, "but Ladies' Hunter has been called, Tom."

Tom went back into the van without a reply and, seconds later, brought Orion saddled and bridled. As he began to tighten the girth, Mrs. Wilson said, "Tom, I don't like to ride down from the van. I told you that this morning. This time you can't use braiding as an excuse, so please bring Orion to me in ten minutes. At the outside course," she added, and marched away.

Lucy was startled as Tom's face twisted with fear. "Tom, Rudi's here with the horses," she said. "All you have to do is walk over there."

Rudi unfolded himself out of the driver's seat. "Kid, you've been up here at the van all day. Kendrick expects to see you helping around. You'll get kicked in the butt if you don't get down there."

Tom looked as though he wanted to turn and run, but he led Orion off in the direction Lucy had pointed.

"Wait, Tom. I'll walk you partway." Holding Peanut's bridle, Lucy grabbed a rag near the van door. "You'll need this to wipe off Mrs. Wilson's boots."

What about her own boots? Before handing over the rag, she gave them each a good rub.

"I'm totaled," Lucy said as she and Debby were slumped in Liz's van.

"But you've had a good day."

"Yeah—I mean yes. Mr. Kendrick said Open over fences was my best ride ever, even if I was out of the ribbons."

"The competition's still too tough, but you're getting there. Wasn't it great that both Liz and Frank placed in the Maclay? And all of our riders had at least one ribbon."

"I'll tell you who else had a good day," Lucy said. "The Hodgsons. Did you see the ribbons across the front of their van?"

"Sure. I guess they do a good job, even if we don't want to think so."

"Don't forget how many of their riders were trained by Mr. Kendrick."

"Be fair, Lucy. How about Dena—the handicapped girl?"

"I'm in no mood to be fair," Lucy said. "I admit it. Mr. Kendrick's had a lot of new problems since that stable opened up. And somehow, today, they all seem intense."

Lucy started to collect her gear. "Maybe Mr. Kendrick will let me go home now. I was going to try to cover for Tom some, but I'm wiped out."

"You've already helped him enough today. What was his problem, anyway?"

"He did everything perfectly at the van, but getting him to leave it was like prying the computer nerds from their Apples."

"You think about Tom a lot."

"Not really. He just puzzles me. I've never known anyone like him."

"Me neither, and we're lucky!"

As she drove home with her parents Lucy curled up in the back of the Toyota, staring blankly out of the window.

"Tired, Mite?"

She sat up straight. "Dad, don't you think it's time to drop that nickname?"

"You don't like it anymore?"

"I'm not three years old. I'd appreciate it if you stopped calling me Mite in front of people."

Mr. Hill made a big display of looking around the car. "There's no one here but your mother and me."

"You *know* you called me Mite in front of everyone today."

"We didn't see John Kendrick," Mrs. Hill said quickly. "Doesn't he come to the shows with you anymore?"

"Mo-om. Of course he comes with us. Who else would come?"

"He has grooms and advanced riders."

"Sure, but he's always there himself. He's just in the schooling area a lot of the time. You must have seen him at the rail during my classes."

"I can't say that I did."

"He was there," Lucy said vehemently.

Lucy knew she was being disagreeable, but she didn't care. She didn't want to talk. She wanted to think about Tom.

Sometimes when her father screened movies at home, a hair would be trapped in the gate of the projector. It would move in and out of the picture frame, often during the whole film. Something was teasing the edge of her mind like that. It was more than just shyness that had kept Tom at the van. He was obviously terrified of being seen. No one really knew very much about him. Could he be in trouble with the police?

"Cheer up, Lucy," her father said. "You'll get that blue next time for sure."

Lucy felt all the emotion of the day burst out at once. "Do you think I'm sulking back here over a ribbon I didn't deserve?" she said. "I've got more important things on my mind. Really! I thought you knew me better than that."

Chapter Five

Tuesday afternoon, after she'd finished with her beginners, Lucy was waiting for Mr. Kendrick in the office, as he'd asked her to. She made halfhearted attempts to study while Carol's jodhpur boots drummed against a wooden chair rail. As usual, some of the kids from her class were hanging around.

"But horses *are* intelligent. They are!" Carol said.

"They're not," Paul insisted. "They just have personality. I read about it."

"If their mothers don't come soon," Sally said through her teeth, "I'll lose my mind."

Lucy looked up from her math book. "Okay, kids. *Outside*. Sunshine's good for you."

"You can overdose on vitamin D."

"Paul, you're a brat. *Out.*"

As the children scuffled through the door, Lucy closed her book. This was the first chance she'd had to talk to Sally since the horse show. On Sunday her mother had insisted she stay home to study for exams, which started this week. Monday the stable was always closed to give the horses a rest.

"I see we're getting a new security system," Lucy said.

"Yes. They've been working on the barn all day. If the kids or anyone else comes breaking in again, an alarm will ring in the police station."

"So everyone still thinks it was the Bolton kids?"

"Of course! Nothing was stolen. Mr. Kendrick checked everything again. The twins were just getting back at him about Eastchester."

"I've been thinking, Sally. We said it had to be someone who knew we were going to a show and who wanted us to look bad."

"You've just described the twins."

"I know. but I've been thinking that the description might fit someone else too." Lucy hesitated. Sally was a good friend. Why not try it? "The braids incident could be part of something bigger."

"Lucy, I don't know what you're talking about," Sally said.

"Look, haven't you heard some of the lies going around about the stable?"

"Have you been getting enough sleep?"

"I'm serious, Sally. I've been hearing talk about carelessness over here, about Mr. Kendrick being different since his wife died . . . you must have heard some of the talk."

"There's always that kind of talk. A parent thinks Mr. Kendrick hasn't given their child enough attention and—"

"This is different. And there's another stable twenty minutes away now. It would be to their advantage to make Mr. Kendrick look bad."

"Lucy Hill, I never knew you had such a devious mind."

"I know it sounds farfetched. At first I thought I

was jumping to conclusions, but new things have happened. I think there's a deliberate campaign—"

"Hold it a minute. Let me think."

Lucy looked at Sally in surprise.

"You know there's a *real* campaign against Mr. Kendrick," Sally said. "For his seat on the Town Council."

"You mean the rumors could have something to do with the election?"

"Could be. Did you see a heavyset man over here about two weeks ago? Drives a blue Cutlass? Well, that's Donald Rupert, a land developer in town. His group on the Town Council wants to build a giant shopping mall in Westlake. A lot of people agree with him—Mr. Bolton, for instance. But Mr. Kendrick and some other of the Council members think the town will lose its character if the shopping mall's approved. They say Westlake's already growing too fast—"

The door whined and Mr. Kendrick looked into the office. "Thanks for waiting, Lucy. Come talk to me while the intermediates assemble."

Lucy waved to Sally and followed Mr. Kendrick into the stable yard.

"School ends in about a week, right?" Mr. Kendrick said.

"Yes." Lucy studied his face carefully.

"Have you made plans for the summer?"

"Uh—the same as always. Why? That's okay, isn't it?"

What was going on? Was this going to be another summer with a problem about a horse? Was Peanuts being shipped out for some reason?

"If you don't have a horse for me to show, I'll just help around," Lucy said weakly.

Mr. Kendrick smiled. "I just thought you might be finding some new diversions now that you're older." He looked at her closely. "Don't be hurt. You're allowed to have options like anyone else."

"I'm as serious about riding as ever. I'm still going to get to the Garden. I'm determined . . . if you'll help me."

"Good! That's what I hoped you'd say. I've been making the summer schedules. Mrs. Kelly had an operation and hasn't been able to ride for a while. Now she and her husband are going to Europe. They've agreed to let you work with Whistle on a regular basis."

Lucy held back a shout. Maybe dreams came true after all!

"I thought you'd be pleased." Mr. Kendrick put an arm over her shoulders. "Finish school. Then we'll get to work. I think both you and the mare will benefit."

For a moment Lucy looked at Mr. Kendrick, unable to think of anything big enough to say. Then he followed a rider to the Indoor Ring and Lucy rushed back to Sally.

"He told me! About me and Whistle! I can't believe it!"

"Isn't it great? I've been biting holes in my tongue not to tell." Sally held up a long white envelope. "I've got another surprise. The mailman just brought this, registered mail. It's the first letter Tom's had since he's been here." Sally pushed the glasses up on her nose. "It's from a Philip Talbot in Houghton Falls, Vermont. That's Tom's hometown."

"Really. I don't know anything about him."

"Mr. Kendrick has a friend who lives up there, Mr. Steiner. Tom used to take care of his horses."

Lucy stretched out on the long bench. "Was there any flack about Tom at the show?"

"Some people were angry he didn't help at the ring more, if that's what you mean."

"He certainly hung around the van."

"He's terribly shy, Lucy. It was his first show, don't forget."

Lucy thought for a moment. "I really got the feeling that he was hiding, Sally. He's not lazy. He was *afraid* to leave the van. I know I have an active imagination." She hesitated. "But suppose Tom's in trouble with the law," she said in a rush. "That would give the Hodgsons or the shopping-mall supporters *real* ammunition against Mr. Kendrick."

Sally looked dazed. "Talk about jumping to conclusions."

"It would be too bad if Mr. Kendrick let him go, but I thought after the show, he might have to."

"No, Mr. Kendrick spoke to Tom and I think he'll keep him for now. Tom's so good with the horses, we may use someone else to help the riders." Sally held up the letter. "Anyway, would you take this to him for me, please?"

Lucy took the letter and started for the door, but the envelope in her hand reminded her of another question.

"By the way, did anyone find out what happened to our missing entries?"

"Of course not," Sally said with irritation. "Blame the U.S. mail. The entries left here two weeks before the show."

"Did you take them to the post office?"

"I don't remember. If someone's going to the village, I hand them the mail. Will you get that over to Tom!"

"Okay, okay."

Crossing the parking area, Lucy studied the envelope. It said "Esquire" after Mr. Talbot's name. Didn't that mean he was a lawyer?

Lucy opened the door to the stable annex at the end of the Indoor Ring and walked past the large box stalls where many of the private horses were kept. There was no one in sight, but she heard a soft voice from Moonrock's stall. Quietly, she moved toward the sound. Tom stood next to the big horse, pouring words against the animal's neck.

"You know that big kid, Eddy Cooper? He's a late starter, but he'll be a great rider if he softens up his hands. Now, the one with the great pair of hands is that Liz, the blond I told you about. She's real pretty, and she's neat. But she doesn't care enough. No drive. Then there's the brown-haired one with the long face." Lucy's cool deserted her. She kicked a tack trunk sharply. The voice stopped.

"Tom, are you there? I've got something for you."

Tom peered over the stall door. Moonrock's large head reached out beside him.

"It's a registered letter."

Tom looked at the envelope in Lucy's hand and quickly stepped back against the horse. The fear in his eyes was chilling. Lucy just stood with her arm outstretched, feeling foolish, until Tom snatched the envelope abruptly. "Okay," he muttered, and slumped back against Moonrock, his eyes now as blank as the rest of his face.

"See you," Lucy said weakly, and walked slowly down the aisle. Suddenly, over the sounds of moving horses and rustling hay, she heard a rhythmic pounding. She followed the noise back to Moonrock's stall. Tom had no idea she was there. With all his strength he was driving his fist again and again into a wooden board of the stall. Lucy caught her breath. Blood trickled from his knuckles. As she walked back to the annex door the pounding of her heart seemed as loud as the sound behind her.

Early Thursday morning Lucy rode her bike to the stable. The long trip would begin to toughen up her legs for a summer on horseback. Exams were over and she had the day off from school. Nothing, not thoughts of Tom, the Hodgsons, or her parents, could bother her today. The clear June weather offered a teasing wind and lavish blossoms brightened the roadside. She pedaled along, steering with one hand and then the other, singing patches of her favorite songs at the top of her voice. Two days of school next week, then vacation and Silver Whistle.

At the crossroad up ahead an antique Model T Ford turned onto the Main Road. As the car chugged along in front of Lucy, the sunlight bounced off its gleaming black paint.

Everyone in town knew that car. It belonged to Henrietta Gibney, publisher of the *Westlaker*. It seemed strange that the publisher of the local news-

paper should drive such an ancient car; what was
more up-to-date than the news? But then, everything about Henny was unusual. I wonder what's up,
Lucy thought. Miss Gibney was always bringing the
news or chasing it.

Even before she reached the stable sign, Lucy
could see the gathering of people beside the Main
Ring. Henny's black Ford was parked nearby. Lucy
forced her tired legs to pedal faster. A short way up
the stable drive she jumped off her bike, stunned by
what she saw.

The jump course was a shambles. Broken rails
hung in pieces. Standards lay smashed on the ground.
Other jumps—the roll top, the stone wall—were
gashed clean through.

Lucy wheeled her bike over to Sally at the ring rail.
"I don't believe this! What happened?"

"Just what you see. The jump course was hacked
up during the night." Sally lowered her voice. "And
now it will be plastered all over today's *Westlaker.*"

Henrietta was standing next to Mr. Kendrick a
short distance away. She really is a character, Lucy
thought. A large wheel of red straw, circled with big
white flowers, was perched on her graying hair. The
ropes of beads spread across her chest were also red
and white. Much of Westlake made fun of Henrietta,
calling her "Henny Penny" or even "the big fat hen,"
but Lucy admired her liveliness and independence.
She'd heard a lot about Henny from her brother Eric,
who'd worked on the paper last summer.

"I'm going to write a big piece, John," Henny was
saying. "These 'town terrors' have got to be

stopped." She scribbled on the oversized pad she carried in a clipboard.

Lucy stared at the ugly scene. Were the Bolton boys still paying Mr. Kendrick back? Or was it just another piece of senseless vandalism? Last week the front of the Jensens' white house had been painted purple in the middle of the night.

"Nobody heard them?" Lucy said to Sally.

Mr. Kendrick noticed her for the first time. "Unless they were yelling and screaming, you wouldn't hear a thing at the barn."

Henny turned to the *Westlaker* photographer. "Have you got your picture? One more and let's go. We've got a deadline to make." Moments later she hurried off, short and plump, her legs moving quickly, as if part of some small windup toy.

Mr. Kendrick called to Jim, who was examining the jumps. "Let's get the truck and move this mess out of here."

"I think there are one or two we can fix," Jim said.

"Leave those, then. For the time being we'll bring some fences from the Indoor Ring." Mr. Kendrick climbed over the ring rail and went to check the roll top with Jim.

Lucy looked after him. Suddenly it was as though one picture on a TV screen were dissolving into another. First she saw the smashed jump course. Then Tom, filled with anger, smashing his bloody knuckles against the stable wall.

Chapter Six

Late that afternoon Lucy slipped out of the Sherman station wagon, one eye on her mother, who was bending over a flower bed across the lawn. She hurried to the front steps and scooped up the folded *Westlaker*. Sure enough, a large photo and a headline broadcast the news: "Jump Course Wrecked at Up and Down Farm."

The picture looked even worse than the real thing. If only there were some way to hide the paper! But of course that was silly.

It had taken quite a while to clear the ruined jumps out of the ring. Meanwhile, each car that pulled up to the stable spilled out people babbling like circus clowns. Finally, Mr. Kendrick had rounded up all the intermediate and advanced riders for a terrific extra lesson in the Indoor Ring.

"Hello, Lucy. Did the *Westlaker* come?" Her father put his head out of the door.

"Yeah, Dad. Here." She folded the paper and handed it over.

"Thanks."

They walked into the house together and Lucy went up the stairs. She heard her mother come in from the garden. "Marion," her father said, "come see the wreck someone made of Kendrick's jump setup."

Lucy flopped down on the bed in her room. What would she do if her parents lost confidence in Mr. Kendrick? She thought back to the afternoon lesson. It had been like an old Western movie when the whole settlement is ordered into the fort. Each rider had tried harder than ever, all banding together against the enemy. Now if only someone could tell her who the enemy was!

"Debby and I thought we'd celebrate the end of exams and go to the movies," Lucy said at the dinner table later. She and Bryan are picking me up at eight o'clock, okay?"

"That's a strange way to ask permission," Mrs. Hill said, "after all the arrangements are made."

"You can go, Lucy," her father said. "Your mother's just being sticky."

"I'm trying to make a point, Allan."

"Sometimes it's better to leave things alone."

"I'm sorry, Mom," Lucy said as brightly as she could manage. "Don't use your veto, *please!*"

"It's all right, Lucy." Mrs. Hill forced a smile. "By the way, Eric phoned. He's going straight from school to the newspaper in Washington. They want him to start a week sooner."

Lucy sighed. "Will he be home at all?" She was sick of being the only buffer between her parents. Besides, she needed someone to really talk to about the stable.

"Probably for a weekend after he gets settled. He'll have a great deal to tell us by then."

"What *I* want to hear about is the situation at Kendrick's," Mr. Hill said, looking at Lucy.

"Allan, not now."

"I guess you saw the evening paper," Lucy said quickly. What a stupid remark. She had handed him the paper herself.

"Look, Lucy, things haven't seemed right over there for some time."

"But, Dad, you're never over there. Everything's as good as it ever was."

"That's not what we've heard," Mrs. Hill put in.

This was great. A minute ago they were tuning up for a fight. Now suddenly it was "we" again and *she* was on the opposite side.

"There was a lot of talk last week at the Eastchester show," her father said.

"Let's be specific, Allan. We've heard that there's stealing at the stable. We've heard that Mr. Kendrick isn't around enough. The people he's hiring aren't of the caliber they used to be."

Lucy was too astonished to answer. Stealing! That was a new one.

"And now somebody's hacking up the place," Mr. Hill added. "All in all it doesn't sound like a spot for someone you care about, does it?"

Lucy put down her fork. She had to get out of here somehow or explode.

"Can I go now—I mean, may I?" She folded her napkin.

"No dessert?" her father said.

"No, thanks."

"She's upset about the stable," Mrs. Hill said as if Lucy were not there.

"Of course she's upset," Mr. Hill said. "But it's not something I can just dismiss. Besides, you added a few coals to the fire yourself."

"I took part in the conversation, if that's what you mean."

Lucy slid out of her seat and left the room.

"Hi, Deb. Hello, Bryan." Lucy climbed into the Shermans' station wagon shortly after eight o'clock. "Liz saw the movie yesterday and she said it was great."

"Good."

"What's the matter?" Lucy said.

"Did you get any flack about the jump course?"

"And how. But they got caught up in arguing and left it in the air. Why? Did you have a hard time?"

Debby looked down at her lap. "Sort of."

"Debby! Not off to the Hodgsons?"

"No, but it's getting close."

"Well, what did they say?"

"Mostly a lot of stuff about Mr. Kendrick's not being the same since his wife died. How would they know anyway? We weren't even back in this country when Mrs. Kendrick died."

"If Mr. Kendrick is so irresponsible, why did he spend a fortune to tighten security at the barn?"

"Dad thinks the problems are inside the security system."

"He started on Tom again?"

"He says this was obviously the work of a weirdo and that Tom's clearly a disturbed person."

"There are a lot of other people around the stable. Why not blame one of them?"

"Who—Liz? Jim? Can't you see Jim hacking jumps in half so he can put them back together again? He's got enough work to do."

"Mr. Kendrick and Henny are convinced it was the twins and some of the other kids who've been raising hell. The problem is proof. I know Mr. Kendrick's been talking to the police."

"Lots of kids at school go in for that kind of stuff. Let's forget it for now."

"Really!"

It looked as though half the school had decided to celebrate the end of exams at the village CINE. Lucy and Debby hurried to find seats, then Lucy went out to the candy stand. She hung back when she saw Scot and Steve Bolton at the counter. Scot was holding two cartons of popcorn while Steve counted out change.

"Hey, Lucy," Steve called, noticing her.

"Hi, guys." She walked to the counter with deliberate cool. "Hey, Lucy," Scot echoed. "I hear someone whacked up Kendrick's fences."

"I'll bet you heard."

"What's that supposed to mean?" Steve asked.

"She's got some kind of a chip on her shoulder," Scot said. "Like at the show. She just about accused us of opening up the braids."

"Come on, Lucy, We felt rotten about the jump course," Steve said.

"Of course we did," Scot said.

Was this some kind of a phony routine? Were they putting her on?

"Yeah, Lucy." Scot added. "We learned to jump over those fences same as you, remember?"

Confused, Lucy looked at her feet.

"Look, we were sorry to leave Kendrick," Steve said. "He did have a point about the smoking."

"Your father didn't think so."

"Guess not," Scot said. "But he was mad at Kendrick already. Mr. K.'s got to get with the times."

"Why?" Lucy protested. "Because he doesn't think horse shows are the whole of riding? Because he hates to see competition take over the sport?"

"Not that so much," Steve said. "It's more about the town standing still."

"What's that got to do with riding?"

"Nothing. But Pop is fed up with trying to make Kendrick see straight. What's wrong with a shopping mall in Westlake? Mr. Kendrick's been running in one place for too long."

"Honestly, you sound like *parrots*, as though every word comes straight from your father."

"So what? He knows what he's talking about," Scot said sharply. "He's a contractor. He's built two terrific shopping malls in Connecticut already. They're good for the towns. They bring in new jobs and more money—"

"Come on, Scot. The picture's starting."

"Yeah."

As Lucy walked down the aisle balancing two cartons overflowing with popcorn, the opening titles were already on the screen. She watched the moving images with only half her mind. So Mr. Bolton built things like shopping malls—*that*'s how he made so much money. Then removing Mr. Kendrick from the

Town Council wasn't just a matter of what was good for Westlake. It might be a question of what was best for Mr. Bolton!

Silver Whistle was the big excitement of the next two weeks and Lucy resolved that sleuthing would have to be put aside. The mare was more than a great ride. Lucy had never known such an affectionate horse. Whistle came to the front of her stall each day at the sound of Lucy's voice. She would lick Lucy's hands and follow behind her without a lead rope. Mr. Kendrick scheduled extra private lessons for Lucy on Whistle, but the mare was a good teacher too. She responded quickly to correct commands and balked just enough when the signals were poor. Every day with the horse was an opportunity and Lucy wasn't going to blow it.

The stable had returned to its usual discipline and calm. There were bright new jumps in the Main Ring now, and police patrolled the stable drive several times a night. As before, Tom was helpful, if silent.

On Friday the Advanced Jumping class was having a particularly good time. Lucy was using Peanuts for a favorite exercise—jumping low fences without stirrups or reins, arms folded behind her back.

"More leg, Eddy. Steer him into the jump with your legs," Mr. Kendrick said, as everyone watched closely.

The horse refused the fence and ran out to one side.

Eddy reached for the reins, knotted on the horse's neck. "Can I use these now, Mr. Kendrick?"

"Just to bring him back. This time keep up the pressure until he jumps."

"Mr. Kendrick," Liz shouted from the Beginners' Ring. "Mr. Kendrick!"

"Hold it, Eddy," In seconds Mr. Kendrick had climbed the fence and crossed the road.

Lucy and Sally brought their horses to the edge of the ring and tried to see why Liz was calling.

"It looks like Warlock's running around without a rider," Lucy said.

"Joey Rose must have gone off. He usually rides Warlock."

Mr. Kendrick reached the other ring and vaulted the fence. The confusion of horses and riders made it impossible to see anything else.

"It can't be too serious," Lucy said. "None of those jumps is even three feet."

"He probably just had the wind knocked out of him," Sally agreed.

Stuart Rogers, one of the eleven-year-olds, ducked under the Beginners' Ring fence and ran toward them.

"Mr. Kendrick says to get Tom and Jim," he yelled. "And Sally's supposed to call the Westlake ambulance." Lucy and Sally looked at each other. The horses took those low fences easily. And even when kids *did* fall off, they were never hurt.

"What happened, Stuart?" Sally asked.

"Warlock tripped on the far side of the fence and rolled on Joey."

"Let's move it," Sally urged. Eddy rushed to the gate and the girls cantered off together across the field. As Lucy turned toward the barn, Jim came running.

"There's been an accident in the Beginners' Ring," Lucy called. "Mr. Kendrick needs you."

"Saw it from the roof. I'm headed down there."

Lucy hurried on and brought Peanuts right into the barn doorway. "Tom," she shouted, "hurry. There's been an accident."

In seconds Tom was running toward the Beginners' Ring, looking like an ostrich as his lanky legs reached far out in front of him. Lucy put Peanuts away quickly and hurried back across the field. On the way she passed Liz's class straggling back to the barn with Jim. Then Sally galloped alongside on Misfit.

"Did you reach the ambulance?" Mr. Kendrick shouted.

"They've already left," Sally called.

In the ring Joey lay on the ground with his eyes closed. Mr. Kendrick and Liz were kneeling beside him. Tom held Warlock.

"Looks like Joey's badly hurt," Sally whispered.

Lucy looked at the jump where the accident had happened. The top rail was still in place. Warlock was sound and surefooted. Why had he tripped? Could his foot have hit a rock? If so, how did it get there?

At the first faint wail of the ambulance Mr. Kendrick stood up, his eyes on the Main Road. "Tom, cold-hose Warlock's foot and wrap it. Otherwise he seems fine. If you have any doubts call Dr. Harris. Liz and I will go to the hospital with Joey. I'll phone his parents from there."

"Suppose you don't reach Mrs. Rose and she comes for Joey here?"

"You'll have to tell her what happened. Joey had a spill, Liz and I took him to Fairmont Hospital, and she should meet us there as soon as possible."

As the ambulance attendants carried Joey from the ring, Lucy saw that the boy was as pale as their white coats. Liz and Mr. Kendrick climbed into the ambulance behind the stretcher and the metal doors closed with a bang. Poor Liz, Lucy thought. It must be hard not to blame yourself if an accident happened while you were teaching—even if you *knew* it wasn't your fault.

"I'm going to put Misfit away and get back to the office." Sally's eyes were blinking hard.

"I'll be up in a minute." Lucy looked over at Tom. He was staring after the ambulance as though no one were around, muttering, "Poor kid, poor kid," and shaking his head.

Lucy walked over to the place where Warlock had rolled. There was no sign of a rock. Of course the dirt and grass were cut up where the horse had scrambled to his feet. But something *did* look odd.

Lucy bent to examine a large piece of turf that was lying in a good-sized hole. It looked as though someone had lifted back a flap of grass, dug a hole, and covered it up again. Several little sticks were lying in the earth. They might have been used to prop up the flap so the ground would look normal.

Sooner or later some horse coming over the jump was bound to put a foot in the hole and trip. In the Beginners' Ring that would mean at least a spill and maybe more. Obviously, someone didn't care, as long as Mr. Kendrick looked bad. Lucy shook her head hard. This was a kind of viciousness she would never understand.

Chapter Seven

Tom hadn't moved from the fence where he'd tied up Warlock. The ambulance had disappeared long ago, but he was still staring after it. As Lucy walked toward the boy, he folded up like a dangling marionette and flopped to the ground. He began to pull at the grass.

Lucy sat down nearby. She said nothing, hoping Tom would start to speak.

"Guess he broke a bunch of bones," Tom said finally, wrapping his thin arms around himself.

"Have you ever broken any bones?"

"Yeah, on the farm. When I was a little kid, most of all." Tom twisted his face and looked off down the road.

"I always wondered where you learned so much about horses. You grew up on a farm, huh?"

Tom nodded.

"Did your father teach you to ride?"

"That's a laugh." The words burst out.

Lucy hesitated. "But there were horses on the farm, right?"

"Yeah. People brought them for us to keep, like here." For the first time he looked straight at her as he talked. "Near where we lived, rich people came with horses in the summer."

"So, do your parents still live there?"

The answer came slowly. "My mother died. I killed her when I was born."

Lucy was horrified. "That's crazy! Things like that just happen." She looked into his face. "It's never the baby's fault. You can't say that."

"My old man said it all the time."

"That's *awful!*"

"He's rotten mean, that's all. I was always in the wrong. He told me so, too. Beat me with anything he could lay his hands on."

Lucy couldn't believe she was hearing these things from someone who'd actually lived through them. It wasn't like the TV news. You understood that the news was happening somewhere in the world, but you could pretend it wasn't real. This was different.

"I don't know much besides horses," Tom suddenly went on. "Seems like I was mucking out stalls soon as I walked. Aunt Audrey, she's my mother's sister, she said I worked like a man before I was up to her waist. She'd fight with him to let me go to school." He fell silent again.

"Can you ride horses as well as you take care of them?"

"Maybe. The summer people taught me after a while. When Mr. Steiner came—Mr. Kendrick's friend—I could ride pretty good. 'I'm going to polish you up, Thomas,' he was always saying. One time I watched the Olympics on Aunt Audrey's TV. Then I saw what he was trying to do. He was trying to teach me to ride like them."

"You were lucky!"

"Yeah, some luck. My father just beat me up more for taking on fancy ways."

Suddenly Tom began to shake. Lucy reached a hand out to his arm, but pulled it back before she touched him. "You know you're okay here. You do know *that*, don't you?"

Tom grabbed at clumps of grass with one bony hand. "They brought me back two times."

"You mean you ran away?" She forced her voice to sound casual. "So what if you did? They can't get you back anymore."

Tom took time to stand up, as though his body hurt. "Guess not." He walked over to Warlock, unhitched the horse from the fence, and left the ring without looking back.

Lucy sat very still. If Tom was under eighteen and a runaway, no wonder he'd stayed out of sight at Eastchester. Some horsey person from his former life might have seen him and told his father. Then back to beatings and abuse. Child abuse wasn't only about dead kids you read about in the paper. Some of those kids grew up, so filled with misery they holed up inside themselves, like Tom.

Tom had reached the head of the drive, leading Warlock with that strange loping walk. Lucy thought how removed his life seemed from hers . . . from name pancakes and shell collections and visits to Grandpa and Grandma Hill in California. Suddenly the space around her seemed frighteningly large, as though the trees at the edge of the fields were blocking her view for miles and miles beyond.

She stood up and stretched out the stiffness in her

legs. She had no right to be afraid. She didn't have to wrap herself in a bubble of silence and unhappiness. She didn't have to talk to horses instead of people. She had two parents who would protect her no matter what.

A red BMW turned into the stable driveway. Lucy could hardly believe the conversation with Tom had pushed Joey's accident so far to the back of her mind. She ran toward the office. She didn't want Sally to have to talk to Mrs. Rose all by herself.

A week later Eric came up from Washington for a few days. Lucy sat next to her brother along the edge of their backyard pool, grateful for the chance to talk to him alone. The sun was almost gone, but even at eight o'clock there was enough heat in the air to let them feel comfortable in wet suits.

"So someone deliberately dug a hole on the far side of the jump and covered it over," Lucy said. "Can you believe that! Sooner or later some horse had to trip."

"Was Joey badly hurt?"

"I heard he broke his leg and his collarbone. He's still in the hospital."

"So, what happened after you saw the hole?"

"I showed it to Sally, and of course she showed it to Mr. Kendrick later."

"What does *he* think?"

"I don't know. He called the police and there's been a detective talking to people around the barn. Maybe now people will realize there's more going on than some kids getting even."

Lucy looked at her brother. As he pushed his wet

black hair off his forehead, he reminded her a lot of their father. His blue eyes were serious.

"What do you think, Luce?"

"That someone is out to get Mr. Kendrick."

"What? What gave you an idea like that?"

"The rumors, to start with. There's been a smear campaign about carelessness at the stable. The picture of the ruined jump course in the *Westlaker* helped it along, and now Joey's accident is the limit. Henny played it down, but of course it was in the paper."

"Henny's great. I've got to get over to see her."

"The Roses won't make trouble for Mr. Kendrick. They're not like that and they've had three children at the stable for years. But Mr. Kendrick's reputation is being hurt and his business too."

Eric shook his head. "I don't get it. Who would go after Mr. Kendrick? He's always been so well liked in Westlake."

"I know, but things change. First of all there's a new stable in Wilmont run by some people named Hodgson—"

"Mom mentioned that. She said they seem okay."

"It's funny. Mom's the one who's always telling us not to judge by appearances. She saw the Hodgsons *once*, over at the Eastchester show. So they're good with their riders, they could still be greedy for business."

"You think they're trying to smear Mr. Kendrick to get business?"

"That's right. New people won't come to him if awful things keep happening. And people have been leaving too."

"Lucy, people who ride with Mr. Kendrick *know* he isn't careless."

"Their parents don't," Lucy said pointedly. "I'm plenty worried that Dad and Mom are going to ship *me* over to Wilmont." She took a breath. "Anyway, that's only one possible answer. Do you remember Mr. Bolton with the twin boys? He's trying to get Mr. Kendrick off the Town Council in the next election—"

"What's Bolton's stake in that?"

"He'd like to see a big shopping mall go up in Westlake. I think he'd like to build it too. He's built a few already."

"And Mr. Kendrick's vote is in the way?"

"You got it."

"Lucy, I can't really see Mr. Bolton digging a hole in the middle of the night . . ."

Eric reached down into the pool and ran his hand back and forth in the water. When he sat up again he said, "Who's working at the barn these days?"

"Two of the older kids, Liz and Eddy, help muck out the stalls and feed the horses. Sally helps in the office and Jim's the new handyman."

"What happened to Nick Walker?"

"He's okay, but he fell off a ladder about a month ago, so he can't work anymore."

"What's the new handyman like?"

"He's nice enough. Full of jokes. You might remember him from when he worked as a handyman at school."

"Tall and thin? Sort of good looking?"

"That's him."

"Isn't there a full-time groom anymore?"

Lucy hesitated. "A guy named Tom, who was hired about five months ago. He's terrific with horses."

"What do you know about *him*? Could he have anything to do with what's happening over there?"

It was such a simple question. But she'd never get Eric to understand why it was so difficult to answer.

"Suppose he had a row with Mr. Kendrick and got angry?" Eric went on. "Could Tom take a hatchet to the jump course?"

"No," Lucy said slowly. "And I'm absolutely sure he wouldn't do anything to hurt a child or a horse. And he wouldn't talk against Mr. Kendrick either. He hardly talks at all."

Eric fell silent. While he thought, he cracked his knuckles the way Lucy hated. "Okay, Tom's good with horses and he doesn't talk much. If the Hodgsons or anyone is really out to get the stable, they could be paying him to make trouble from the inside."

"Wow. That's some idea," Lucy said. "But Tom wouldn't. He's no good at pretending."

Eric looked at her thoughtfully. "How old is this guy?"

"Don't be stupid. I don't like him *that* way."

"How old is he, Pigface?" When Lucy was little, "Pigface" always meant "Give it to me or else."

Lucy scowled and slipped back into the water. She bobbed up and down a few times, then came back to Eric and hung on the side of the pool. This was no time to be touchy. Eric could really help.

"Around eighteen, something like that. Anyway,

he looks eighteen. He's had a terrible life. I've never met anyone so hurt."

"Hurt?"

"I can't tell it to you just like that. It wasn't easy to hear. His father used to beat him and keep him out of school and make him work too hard."

"I guess he knows how to talk after all, if he told you all that."

Lucy's stomach tightened. "Don't be mean, Eric." She climbed out of the pool and grabbed the towel on the umbrella table. She rubbed her hair dry, trying to keep her cool.

"Look, Tom never talked at all until the last few weeks. But when Joey went off in the ambulance, he broke down and told me the whole story." She tossed the towel on the table and sat beside Eric again.

"Lucy, listen to me," Eric said patiently. "Tom could have a police record. He could be acting out all kinds of things over there."

"He's not like that, Eric. Believe me. Come to the stable and meet him. Tom's been hurt, that's all—too hurt to harm other people, especially kids." Lucy stood up abruptly but her brother reached for her bathing suit strap and pulled her back down beside him.

"That's not the way it works, Mite."

"Don't you call me Mite. That's Dad's name. You're just a kid, too."

Eric took a deep breath. "Lucy, I'm no expert, but I have studied some of this in psych class. Most victims of child abuse become abusers themselves. They're not kinder and gentler with their own kids. They've only known abuse and they give it back."

Lucy felt sick to her stomach. The phone on the screen porch jangled loudly. Grateful for the interruption, she ran to answer. Maybe Eric knew the statistics, but he didn't know Tom.

Sally's voice leapt from the phone. "The stable's on fire. We need all the help we can get."

Chapter Eight

Shivers ran through Lucy's body as they drove to the stable. "This can't be happening," she said, though she could already smell smoke. "Hurry, Eric, please!"

"I don't dare go any faster. Look at the speedometer."

"I should have asked Sally some questions—if all the horses are okay, whether it was the main barn or the Indoor Ring . . ." Lucy leaned against the dashboard as if trying to push the car forward. Her legs felt cold.

A siren wailed in the distance. "If the firemen are just getting there, the whole stable could be gone," she said.

Eric patted her shoulder. "Maybe it's an ambulance."

"That's even worse. Hurry!"

At the bend in the Main Road Lucy rolled down the window and strained to see across the fields. Thick black smoke billowed over the north end of the barn.

"How could this have happened?" Lucy said. "No electric appliances are allowed in the barn—not even a soda machine—and all the wiring was just checked when the new security system went in."

"Someone could have dropped a cigarette—or torched the place."

"You mean on purpose? Who would do that?"

"Who would hack up a jump course?"

Eric pulled the car onto the field near the paddock and Lucy jumped forward on the seat. "Peanuts is okay!" she said, pointing to the stocky brown horse tied there. Eddy was moving among other horses, hitching head ropes to the fence.

"I don't know what I'll do if any horses are hurt."

"Come on, Luce. Calm down."

They pushed their way through the crowd of strangers gathered in the roadway.

For a moment, when they got closer to the barn, the squealing of terrified horses made Lucy unsteady on her feet. Firemen hurried past with hatchets and pikes. A large hose was aimed at the North Wing and two men braced themselves to hold the nozzle. A torrent of water splashed against huge spikes of flame. From another engine a second hose wet down the hayloft. Police cars and an ambulance were parked near the office. At the South-Wing door Liz and Frank struggled to lead a horse away from the barn.

Lucy broke away from Eric and ran toward Sally, who was arguing with a fireman.

"I've got to get to him," she shouted. "Misfit won't listen to anyone but me. Who can I talk to?"

"The Chief over there. He's in charge, miss."

"I tried that. He won't let me near."

"Where's Mr. Kendrick?" Lucy asked Sally.

"He's been working with the firemen to get the

horses out. But Misfit's no thoroughbred hunter or grand prix jumper. No one cares about *him!*"

"Sally, what about Tom? Is he safe? I don't see him."

"He's safe, all right. He skipped town."

"What?"

"One of the policemen saw him hitching on the Post Road."

"Maybe he just went to a movie."

"Who cares about him. I want Misfit out of there."

"They'll get him, Sally. It looks like things are under control."

An enormous crash covered Lucy's words. Flames sliced through the end wall of the North Wing as if from a giant blowtorch.

"My God, Lucy." Sally sobbed. "He'll be overcome by smoke and they'll never drag him out." Lucy herself was trying not to cry at the desperate sounds from the trapped horses.

"Bring the horses out through the South Door," the Chief shouted into his bullhorn. "We need another line over here fast. Take the horses out of the Indoor Ring."

Lucy's eyes smarted and tears were forming in the corners. As she looked around for Eric, she saw Liz crossing to the annex.

"Liz," she called, "is Shogun safe? And how about Whistle?"

"Shogun's out already," Liz shouted. "Come on. The wind's changing and they're afraid of sparks hitting the Indoor Ring. Help us get the horses out."

"What about Whistle?"

"Watch it, Lucy," Eric said, passing by with Redford. Great, Lucy thought. Debby's horse was okay.

Lucy ran after Liz. "Please, Liz. Where's Whistle?"

"They had her halfway out when she bolted back
into her stall. She's panicked in there. No one can get
near her."

"But *I* can. I've got to!" As Lucy rushed back to
the barn, Mr. Kendrick's head appeared at the
South-Wing door. He wore a mask over his face and
an oxygen tank on his back.

"Mr. Kendrick," she yelled. "I can get Whistle out,
I know it. Please, Mr. Kendrick." There was no sign
that he'd heard.

Lucy turned at the screech of Dr. Harris's van pulling up to the front of the office. The veterinarian
sped by her, calling, "Where's Kendrick? Where are
you, John?"

Behind him Sally slipped past the fire chief and ran
for the barn door. Lucy moved quickly to block her
path.

"Sally, listen to me. *Please.* Go back to the office.
Wait there."

There was a patch of dried blood on Sally's lip
where she'd bitten too hard. The whites of her eyes
were streaked with red.

"Go on, Sally," Lucy pleaded, and headed her toward the office door. "I'll bring you bulletins. I promise."

Lucy watched Sally walk off like a robot. Then she
turned back to the barn. At that second Orion ex-
ploded through the South door. Plunging and snort-
ing, he tossed off the jacket that was covering his
head. Mr. Kendrick struggled to hold on to his halter.

"Take him, someone."

Frank and Eddy rushed for the horse, but the animal kicked and wheeled. He wrenched out of Mr. Kendrick's grasp and turned back toward his stall. As the boys grabbed for him, he wheeled again and bolted across the parking area.

Two firemen leapt onto an engine. Another jumped into Dr. Harris's van. As the horse pounded toward the paddock, Liz and Eric moved to the side of the road. Orion galloped on as though running the Kentucky Derby.

At that moment Lucy saw Debby's station wagon approaching on the Main Road. What would happen when the car met the onrushing horse in the stable drive? But the car didn't turn in. Instead, Bryan pulled straight across the roadway, blocking Orion's path. The horse charged toward them, and for a moment it looked as if he would jump right over the car. But all of a sudden he veered off to the fields. In seconds Debby and Bryan were after him, shouting and throwing clumps of dirt to change his direction. Finally Frank and Eddy reached the bottom of the field and Orion was surrounded.

Mr. Kendrick's voice nearby brought Lucy's attention back to the stable yard. He was talking to a tall fireman whose soot-covered face was streaked with perspiration.

"We've got to make another try for the gray mare," Mr. Kendrick was saying. "That part of the barn's holding. Do you think Lucy could—"

"She'll be safe, John," the fireman interrupted. "We've soaked that section of the barn and checked the walls on each side. She'll wear a mask and I'll be right beside her."

Lucy stepped closer. Water drenched her sleeve as a hose changed position. "Please Mr. Kendrick. I'll be all right. I'll do just what he says."

Mr. Kendrick paid no attention. "Nothing doing, I can't let her go in there. My idea was to let her calm the horse through the outside window while I tried to approach from the inside."

Lucy plunged into the barn. "Come back here!" Mr. Kendrick shouted behind her. She moved up the aisle, crouching under a haze of smoke. Her eyes stung. Her nostrils filled with the smells of charred wood and leather. She held her wet sleeve against her nose. Approaching Whistle's stall, she began to murmur, "Where are you, Whistle? It's all right, baby. I'm going to get you out of here."

The mare was thrashing around in the stall, knocking herself from one wall to the other. "Whistle, baby," Lucy crooned, "come on, girl. Come to Lucy." The mare's ears cocked. She was listening. The smoke was getting thicker. Lucy began to cough and choke.

"Take a deep breath." The fireman held his mask over her face. She wondered if Mr. Kendrick was behind him. She wouldn't think about it now.

Lucy inhaled deeply, then pushed the mask away. She began to edge closer as the mare quieted down. Suddenly, Whistle took several steps toward Lucy. Lucy grabbed the halter and kept talking. At the same time she urged the horse out of the stall.

As they moved toward the aisle, Lucy was face to face with Mr. Kendrick.

"Can you handle her from here?" the fireman asked. "Do you want us to help?"

"I'm okay. She might bolt if you come too close."

With Mr. Kendrick in front and the fireman alongside, Lucy led the mare out of the barn. "Take Whistle," Mr. Kendrick shouted at the doorway, and Dr. Harris rushed over. Lucy told her trembling legs to behave. Suddenly Mr. Kendrick grabbed her shoulders. He turned her toward him and looked her straight in the eye.

"Lucy, I make the decisions around here and you know it. You could have been killed!"

Lucy looked at her feet. She forced her eyes back up to Mr. Kendrick's face. "I know," she whispered, expecting the words to sound louder. "I just—"

"There's no excuse. None. A move like that again and—"

She couldn't answer. Another fireman hurried over. "We need you, John, with the brown horse in the outside stall."

"Right." Mr. Kendrick turned back to Lucy. "Do you understand? Answer me."

She gulped. "Yes, Mr. Kendrick."

"Now, run and tell Sally we're going in for Misfit."

Mr. Kendrick was looking at her sternly, but his eyes softened as he turned away. Lucy stared after him blankly, her body completely numb. Then she shuddered and was back in control.

Dodging the fire trucks and police cars, Lucy crossed to the office and opened the door. Sally was slumped over the oak desk with her head on her arms. As the door whined, she looked up slowly, staring at Lucy with glazed eyes. For a moment something about Sally's despair reminded Lucy of Tom. Where *was* he, anyway? She walked over to the desk and said gently, "Sally, Mr. Kendrick's going after Misfit now."

"I think I'd rather wait in here. He's probably dead anyway."

"I don't think so."

"Just come back and tell me what happens."

Lucy waited, wishing she could comfort Sally, but there was nothing to do.

"Go on!" Sally said.

At the South-Wing door Misfit stretched out his head as though it were just any day and he were searching for carrots. Lucy burst out laughing. The comic relief was welcome, but then she looked more closely. Wheezing and coughing, the horse stumbled as Mr. Kendrick led him from the barn. Dr. Harris hurried over, trailing a small green canister on wheels. He took the horse as Mr. Kendrick went back into the barn.

"Lucy, watch the oxygen so no one knocks it over."

Dr. Harris's hand went to the pulse in Misfit's throat. Then he grabbed the oxygen mask on the top of the canister and covered the animal's face. Lucy watched Misfit's difficult breathing, feeling that her own breaths were just as labored.

At last Dr. Harris removed the mask. He pressed his finger against the horse's gum and took it away, watching the speed at which the color returned.

"You can get Sally," he said. "There's some smoke inhalation damage, but if the horse takes it easy for a few days, he'll be fine."

Lucy raced for the office. Seconds later she

watched Sally throw herself on Misfit's neck. The shower of pet names made Lucy grin. She felt herself begin to relax. All the horses were out. Eric ran toward her smiling.

"Looks okay, Lucy. Some close calls but no casualties. By the way, where is this Tom you were talking about?"

The reminder came as a jolt. I can't kid myself anymore that he's coming back, Lucy thought. He would have been here by now.

"I haven't seen him."

"I thought he slept at the barn."

"He does. I mean, he's supposed to." Lucy was grateful that Eric let the matter drop.

Chapter Nine

It was after ten o'clock when Lucy finally looked at her watch. People had stopped running back and forth in the stable yard and were beginning to chat in groups. Two firemen were folding a hose and Henny had finally cornered the Chief. They made a funny picture—the tall man in the black rubber helmet talking to the short woman in a big straw hat. That hat with a green print dress and matching beads was a strange outfit for covering a fire. Lucy walked over to Henny hoping to hear how the fire had started.

". . . in the North Wing tackroom," the Chief was saying, "as near as we can make out."

"Who turned in the alarm?" Henny asked.

"Some man who wouldn't leave his name."

Henny looked up from her oversized pad. "The alarm was turned in by an unidentified man! You've no idea who it was?"

"No idea."

Henny paused and one hand began to play with her beads. "Of course there were sprinklers in the barn," she said. "Why didn't they work?"

"You can bet John Kendrick's asking the same

question." The Chief took off his helmet and rubbed his forehead. "Bad luck, this whole thing. But John had some good luck too. There wasn't much wind. And the stable was waiting for hay. What little they had was all stacked up at the South end."

"Lucy, dear, would you like a cold drink?" Gratefully, Lucy accepted a cup of juice from Liz's mother. By now many of the stable family were arriving. The doughnut a father offered was welcome too.

As Lucy drained the paper cup, she caught sight of Mr. Kendrick. He stood by himself at the edge of a light spill so that she saw his face in fragments—one bloodshot eye, a thin line of mouth in a blackened cheek. The reality of the fire suddenly hit her full force. It wasn't just the damage to the barn and the tack. The gossip, the stories, and photographs in the newspaper, could be even worse.

Lucy walked toward Mr. Kendrick, but Dr. Harris got there first. "I've double-checked the horses that had the hardest time," Lucy heard the vet saying. "They're all going to be fine. Wish I could say the same for the barn."

Mr. Kendrick breathed a long sigh. Turning to survey the damage, the men walked out of earshot. A few words floated back to Lucy. "Sarge saw him . . . the Fairmont Highway." I'm doing a lot of eavesdropping, Lucy thought as she followed behind them, but I don't care!

"By now people know about the fire all the way to Hartford," Mr. Kendrick was saying. "He should have been back." There was a long silence.

"He's the best you've had with the horses in years, but I've got to say he's a strange one." Dr. Harris

waved his hand across the ugly sight in front of them.
"Are you thinking he had something to do with this?"

The entire North Wing of the barn was rubble and
smoldering wood. In the charred cavity that had
been the tack room, two firemen were wetting down
the ashes and crumbled cement. The Chief came up
to Kendrick.

"Looks like you've lost the tack room and ten stalls,
maybe eleven. And of course, the apartment. Sorry,
we did our best."

There's no one to sleep in the apartment anyway,
Lucy thought. Had Tom discovered the fire and
taken off, afraid he'd be blamed? Could the fire have
been his fault? He smoked a lot. Maybe he'd been
careless with a cigarette. Or could he possibly have
set the fire on purpose?

Lucy forced her mind away from the subject.
Where was Debby anyway? She went to look for her
in the paddock.

The overhead lights in the paddock shone down
on the twenty-nine horses, all fenced in together.
Horses were tied all around the enclosure. Others
stood dazed at the center or dashed back and forth
in sudden spurts. Debby and Frank were checking
hitch knots and preventing trouble.

As Lucy climbed the fence, Superman trotted toward her. A short piece of frayed rope dangled from
his halter. The excited animal was hardly recogniz-
able as the docile old fellow of the Beginners' Ring.
Lucy petted him, then hurried to Whistle, tied up at
the north end. Stroking the mare's face, Lucy
scanned the paddock. She spotted Peanuts . . . Orion
. . . Redford . . . but where was Moonrock?

Eddy and Debby joined Lucy. "What a night," Debby said. "I'm beat, but **completely**." Everyone looked back at the barn. It seemed as though a gigantic monster had come out of the darkness, chewed a piece out of one side, and turned away.

"Where were you when Sally called?" Debby asked.

"I was taking the garbage out in my bare feet," Eddy said. "I grabbed the car keys and ran. See?" He looked down at his scratched and bloodstained feet.

"You're lucky you have toes," Debby said, "after working around horses all night like that!"

"Has anyone seen Moonrock?" Lucy's eyes moved up and down the paddock.

"Shouldn't you ask, 'Has anyone seen Tom?'" Eddy said coolly.

"They don't necessarily go together," Lucy snapped.

"Tom's gone, isn't he? Suppose he set the fire to get at Mr. Kendrick for some reason. He could have turned Moonrock loose before he took off."

Lucy felt her eyes get hot. She called out to Liz, who was walking toward them. "Have you seen Moonrock?"

"Sure," Liz said. "I brought him down from the annex myself. He was tied up over there near Redford."

"He isn't there now." Lucy climbed up onto the paddock fence and checked the ring again. At least the horse had been there after Tom took off. That was a relief! Maybe he'd broken loose, like Superman, and then jumped the fence. Or maybe he'd been stolen in the confusion. There'd been a lot of strangers around all night.

Sally came running from the barn. "Mr. Kendrick says to start bringing the horses up. We're putting them into the Indoor Ring for the night."

"No rest for the weary." Liz sighed, untying the horse nearest her.

But what about Moonrock, Lucy thought. He was the finest hunter Mr. Kendrick ever owned.

"Come on, Lucy," Eddy said, opening the gate. "We've got twenty-nine horses to move."

"You're not listening, Eddy," Lucy said. "There're only twenty-eight." But he was already too far away to hear.

The search began as soon as Mr. Kendrick learned that Moonrock was missing. Debby left in a police car, Henny took off in the Model T Ford. Along with some of the other stable regulars, Lucy waited for instructions in the office. Sally was busy at the coffee maker, once again calm and helpful. Mr. Kendrick sat behind the oak desk clutching a mug of black coffee.

"Eric and Liz, suppose you take the big flashlight and search the fields. We'd better set a curfew." Mr. Kendrick twisted to the clock on the wall. "Ten thirty. Come back by midnight."

"How about us?" Lucy asked.

"Suppose you and Eddy walk the trail. Be back by midnight too."

At the screen door Lucy turned to look at Mr. Kendrick. His faced sagged with exhaustion as he stared into his coffee cup, but his back was straight and his shoulders squared.

This was Lucy's first time out on the trails late at night. The familiar woods were mystical in the moonlight, the branches darkened, the leaves touched with silver.

"Do you hear something, Eddy?"

"Yes. Wait."

"Darn. It's some small animal like a raccoon. It's not enough noise for a horse."

"Come on. We'd better walk faster," Eddy said.

"My feet won't go any faster."

"Yeah. It's been some night."

"I suppose you think Tom's to blame for it all too," Lucy said.

"Huh?" He turned and looked at her.

"Tell me honestly what you think about Tom."

"Oh, him. Look, Lucy, what is there to say? We're dragging our feet out here and Mr. Kendrick's eating his heart out and it's on account of him, right?"

Lucy was too tired to answer. As they trudged along silently, she stared at the moon, visible for a moment above the trail. It looked as though someone had tossed a giant Frisbee into the sky. The full moon was supposed to bring out the wildness in disturbed people. Tom was a disturbed person. Wasn't that the point Eric had tried to make?

Seconds later clouds moved in front of the moon, making the woods dark and eerie. Lucy commanded her feet to move one step and another, and then another.

"Lucy, don't be mad. Talk to me. You asked me what I thought!"

"I'm not angry, Eddy. I'm just miserable. Everything aches. And—and—I got to know Tom a little."

"Like his last name?"

"Oh, shut up."

Eddy pushed aside a branch that was blocking the trail. "Come on. I'm holding it for you."

"Don't do me any favors."

Why was Eddy leading the way, anyhow? She was perfectly capable of going first. Of course he was four years older. He was probably sorry he wasn't paired with Liz. Then it would have been romantic out here in the moonlight. What was the point of walking the trail, anyway? The horse wasn't out there. Sometimes Mr. Kendrick expected too much.

By the time they turned back, Lucy's eyes were beginning to close. Suddenly the craziest idea popped into her head. She started to giggle and she couldn't stop. What if Moonrock had left for the Hodgsons, too?

"It's a quarter to twelve," Eddy announced as they recrossed the wooden bridge. "We'll be back in plenty of time." Lucy looked down at the water, amazed at how much lower the brook was now, in the middle of July, than it had been six weeks before. A lot had happened since she'd rushed out to see the broken board. In fact, she'd just about forgotten the bridge incident altogether.

"I wonder if anyone was luckier than us," Eddy said.

"Let's hope." As soon as they stepped out onto the North field, Lucy looked in the direction of the barn.

The fire trucks and the ambulance were gone, but there seemed to be a large number of people in front of the office.

"Come on," Lucy said with a rush of energy, and they raced across the field to the edge of the crowd.

Quickly, Lucy worked her way to the front of the group. Mr. Kendrick was the center of attention, holding Moonrock's halter. Next to him Lucy saw a pleasant-looking man with a blond mustache and a slender woman with a blond braid down her back.

Mr. Kendrick made room for Lucy beside him and threw an arm around her shoulder.

"You've got him back!" Lucy exclaimed.

"Sure have. The Hodgsons were driving back from Stamford and found him on the road. Have you met Mr. and Mrs. Hodgson, Lucy?" He turned to the couple beside him. "This is Lucy Hill, one of my special girls." Mr. Kendrick gave the big horse a loving slap on the rump. "What a night to go out on the town! Haven't we had enough trouble around here?"

"We'd be glad to stable a few horses till you get straightened out," Mr. Hodgson said.

"We could lend you some tack too," Mrs. Hodgson added.

Lucy moved away quietly, her feet dragging against the dirt road. The smell of smoke and charred wood made her nose sting. It would be hard to go on believing that the Hodgsons were behind the troubles at the stable. They were decent people. Even if they'd criticized the stable they wouldn't have dug a trap or started a fire. They wouldn't even have paid anyone to do these things. Lucy reached the Beginners' Ring and gripped the fence, too tired to control.

her tears. She felt as young as when she'd first set foot in the ring. All these years the stable had been a protected place away from the rest of the world. It had been a special territory where she could feel safe and happy while growing up. But the stable sign no longer marked a boundary. Unfairness and ugliness had found a way in.

A car motor stopped behind her. Lucy rubbed a sleeve across her eyes as Eric spoke at her shoulder.

"Come on, Lucy. Let's head home."

"Were you up at the barn?"

"Yes. At least the Rock is back."

"Did you see the Hodgsons?" She felt as though her voice were coming from underwater.

"Yes."

"Do you think—just maybe—they could have brought the horse back as a cover-up?"

"No. They really don't seem like that. Besides, how did they get him in the first place? Big Rock broke his halter and jumped the fence. Kendrick found the leather pieces after the horses were put away. Come on, Luce—home."

He turned her around and shoved her gently toward the car. Neither of them said a word, but she knew they were thinking the same thing. If the Hodgsons weren't responsible for the misfortunes at the stable, the most likely suspect was Tom. He was gone, wasn't he? Why else had he run away?

Chapter Ten

"Say, Dad. There's a Dalmatian, like the stable dogs, only this one is smaller."

Lucy was sitting at an editing table in her father's cutting room in New York City. As the film of a dog-food commercial moved through a series of spools and sprockets from one side of the table to the other, the picture appeared on a small screen at the back. Her father was working with his assistant at another editing machine across the room.

"Isn't she a beauty?" Mr. Hill said. "But wait until you see some of the other breeds in the dog-show scene."

Lucy watched the reel to the end. It was a laugh to look at pictures without sound, particularly when you saw dogs barking in every shot. Lucy was pleased that her father had suddenly invited her to his office. After three days of rehashing the fire and arguing about Tom, she welcomed the relief. Everyone at the stable was certain that Tom had been responsible for all Mr. Kendrick's troubles and that now they would end. She'd thought it over and she would bet every blue ribbon on her lampshade that Tom was innocent. Okay, so the Hodgsons were in the clear. But she still had strong suspects left and she was going to keep looking.

"I like the third take," her father said finally. "The guy looks more natural. He holds the food bowls at a better height. The rhythm is better. It's just better." He slid off the metal stool. "Okay, Lucy. Let's you and me get some food. I've made a reservation at a special new place where you've never been."

"Okay, Dad." Lucy tried not to look disappointed. Going to Lindy's was a favorite part of visits to her father's office. They'd memorized all the jokes on the menu. She'd been looking forward to the pickles all morning.

"You're not happy. I can tell." He looked at her closely. "We'll go to Lindy's." He led into their routine. "Customer: 'There's a fly in my soup.' "

Lucy hammed up her answer. "Don't worry. How much soup can a fly drink?" Lucy wondered why he was so anxious to please. She thought a moment. It was her turn to start the joke. "We have everything on the menu today, sir."

"I noticed," her father answered. "Now give me a clean one." They laughed together and Mr. Hill turned to his assistant. "Please cancel for me at Minotte. We're off to our favorite stomping ground."

Boy, was he trying hard. Lucy had an uncomfortable thought. Was this lunch going to be about him and Mom?

"So what did you think of the footage? It has that Al Hill razzle-dazzle, wouldn't you say? Plenty of sparkle?"

"Sure, Dad. Always." Lucy bit the end off another pickle and leaned back against the wooden booth.

"But you know, honey, I'm tired of directing films on responsible dog ownership for pet-food companies, and glamour shots that star a computer. I've got to make a move toward other things—bigger films, bigger money . . ."

"I've heard you and Mom talking about it."

"Arguing about it, I'll bet."

"Yeah, that too."

"I thought Mom told you not to say 'yeah.' "

"Yeah." They both laughed, glad to relieve the tension.

"Mite, I'm going to California."

"You mean for a trip?"

"In a way. But a long trip, maybe six months. You can come visit me out there. It will be fun."

Lucy picked up another pickle and gobbled it down, bite after bite.

"I know this is hard for you, but I'm finally going to do a series for TV. It's my chance, Lucy. A breakthrough into a different kind of film. I've worked for it a long time."

"Mom and I could come with you."

"Not really. You have school, for one thing."

"There are schools in California." She looked him straight in the eye.

"Lucy, you know Mom and I aren't getting along. While I'm out on the Coast, we can try living apart. Mom can try that better life she's always talking about. She can go back to work and do some things she especially likes—get to more theater and concerts—I haven't had enough time for things like that lately."

Lucy bit into another pickle.

"Aren't you going to get sick if you keep on eating pickles like that?"

Lucy said nothing. She didn't need to hear any more of this.

"Dad," she said abruptly, "some people are trying to get Mr. Kendrick off the Town Council because he's against the shopping mall. Are you for or against?"

Mr. Hill pushed his plate away. Her mother hated him to do that. "Look, Lucy, changing the subject won't change the facts. Mom and I have tried to work things out. You know that. We're just too different."

"Differences are interesting."

"Sure, but these differences come up every move we make. It's not interesting anymore. It's irritating and frustrating."

Lucy bit into another pickle. Her father reached over and moved the bowl. "I can't let you eat any more of those. You'll be sick for sure."

"Why are you worrying about me all of a sudden? Pickles just give people stomachaches. If you're going to worry about me, stay in New York." She felt tears in her eyes.

"Lucy . . . Mite . . . don't mix things up. You mean more to me than anyone in the world."

"You don't have to say things like that."

"No. But it so happens I mean them. Trust me. And trust Mom too. You'll still have us both."

"Does Eric know about this?"

"Not yet. I'm going to Washington this weekend to tell him."

"How come you're elected? Did Mom know you were telling me all this today?"

"More or less."

"She certainly didn't let on when she drove me to the station."

"We didn't want to tell you now, when you've just had such a rough time at the stable. But after the weekend with Eric, I've only got two days . . ."

Lucy stopped listening. She felt as though heavy weights had been hung from her shoulders, like those in the grandfather clock in the front hall. Her mother said the right name was a "tall case" clock, but what did she care? Right now she didn't care what either of them had to say about anything.

"Dad, I think I'd like to go to the train from here."

He looked as though she'd slapped him. "Sure. Whatever you like. It's all right. I've got a lot of work to do."

Lucy picked at the bits and pieces that had fallen out of the sandwich onto her plate.

"I'll have the check," her father said to the waiter brusquely. He took a deep breath. "Maybe you'll get back in time for a ride. Are things shaping up over there?"

"Sure. We're even going to a show next Sunday. Mr. Kendrick says we've got to keep the flag flying."

"Guess that's a good idea all around." He reached for the check. Usually he went over the addition, but today he signed without looking. "If you leave now you can get the two-oh-five."

"Yeah—yes. Thanks, Dad." Her father looked so

sad that Lucy wanted to put her arms around him in front of everyone. "I love you, Dad, you know. And thanks for telling me yourself."

"Yes, Mite. I *do* know." He tossed the napkin on the table. "See you tonight. I'll be around until the weekend."

If he had to leave, why didn't he do it fast, like pulling off adhesive tape? Lucy made herself stand up.

"I'll put you in a cab for the station," her father said.

"I can get one myself."

"Listen, Lucy, please." He followed her to the street. "We'll have lunch in California next, you'll see. And you can phone me anytime you want. I'll phone you too."

"Okay, Dad." She kissed him quickly and stepped into a cab as he held the door. The cab pulled into traffic and Lucy turned to look at her father through the back window. He was still standing at the curb watching her drive away.

Lucy stared out of the train window, seeing nothing. Why was it taken for granted that she would live with her mother? Maybe she'd rather go with her father. No, she wouldn't want to leave Mr. Kendrick. But suppose her mother moved to New York as she often talked about? That would mean leaving the stable anyway.

Lucy's mind switched to Tom. If he'd caused the fire by accident, leaving the stable was his big mistake. Maybe he'd been smoking in his apartment. But he should have stayed and faced Mr. Kendrick. Of course, he'd been too afraid.

People had been leaving the stable all week. Some of them had finally lost confidence in Mr. Kendrick. Others wanted to avoid the inconveniences caused by the fire. At this rate Mr. Kendrick might even have to sell the farm!

As the train jolted from one side to the other, Lucy felt as though her brains were shaking into place. She'd thought about the damage to Mr. Kendrick's business . . . his reputation too. But she'd never been able to take the next step—selling Up and Down Farm. Could this be the explanation for the summer's troubles at the stable? Was someone trying to force Mr. Kendrick to sell his property? Who could that be and why?

Suddenly, Lucy couldn't get to Westlake fast enough. There was something she had to find out. Maybe she could still help Mr. Kendrick. Maybe she could still clear Tom's name, even if she never saw him again.

Mrs. Hill had pulled the car alongside the station platform so that Lucy spotted her right away. She slid into the seat beside her mother.

"Daddy called," Mrs. Hill said.

"I figured that when I saw you here."

"He said that he told you."

"Uh-huh."

"About his plans to go to California."

"I knew that's what you meant."

They drove under the railroad bridge and out toward the Post Road.

"There's something I want to say, Lucy. Please listen."

"Mom, I can't. I just can't! Too much is happening at once."

"I'm trying to help."

"I know, Mom. But not now, *please*. Let's talk some other time."

Mrs. Hill took a deep breath and said nothing.

"Mom, could you drop me at Town Hall? I'll walk to the stable from there."

"The Town Hall? What are you up to, Lucy?"

"I just want to check out something. It's harmless. Honest."

"Honey, don't get into something that's not your business. You've enough to think about right now."

"It's about Up and Down Farm, Mom. That's a big part of my life too."

"Of course, but I don't see how you can help." Her mother motioned toward the backseat. "The *Westlaker*'s back there. It talks about the groom who disappeared."

Lucy grabbed the paper. A lead story was headlined: "Police Alert for Westlake Groom Suspected of Arson." The story of the fire was recapped under a photo of the damaged barn. Shaken, Lucy looked up as her mother made the turn that would take them to the Town Hall.

"Suppose I put the car in the parking lot," Mrs. Hill said as she pulled up to the red brick building. "I'll do an errand and meet you back at the car."

"Thanks, Mom," Lucy said, smiling. "I'll tell you about it soon, I promise."

Lucy climbed the steps two at a time and walked into the large central lobby. Gold letters on crinkled glass identified the Hall of Records. The door closed behind her with a bang; embarrassed, she looked around the bare room quickly. No one was there except a stout woman with thinning brown hair, typing behind a counter.

"Hello," Lucy said, with deliberate assurance.

The woman looked up. "Hello. Can I help you?"

"Uh—I hope so. My name's Lucy Hill. We live on King's Road. Do you know Up and Down Farm out on the Westlake Main Road? I'm trying to find out who owns the fields on either side?"

"All right, Lucy. That should be easy."

Lucy's mind raced forward. Joey's accident and the fire had suggested a strong motive at work. And every single incident could have been connected. She began to make a mental list. First came the rumors, then the accident on the bridge . . . the braids . . . the lost entries. Then the damage to the jump course and the bad press. Finally—

"Lucy."

"Sorry. I was miles away."

"I have the information you wanted." The woman handed Lucy a slip of paper with pencil notations. "It took a few extra minutes because both parcels changed hands five months ago. They used to be owned by two different people. Now they both belong to the Wilmont Development Corporation."

"But the property's in Westlake!"

"Even so, that's the name on our records," the woman said pleasantly.

"And who owns the company?"

"It's a private corporation. You can find out by writing to the state attorney general or to the company directly. I've given you the address."

Lucy looked at the slip and put it in her shirt pocket. The address was a Westlake post office box, number 171.

"Well, thank you. Thanks a lot."

As she walked to the parking lot, Lucy's mind was working hard. The fields had changed hands five months ago. The problems at the stable had started about three months ago. Both fields now belonged to the same company, and Mr. Kendrick's land was in the middle. She was onto something, for sure. It certainly looked as though Mr. Kendrick was being squeezed off his land. But who was putting on the pressure? She had to find out who owned Box 171 and right away—before anything else happened at the stable.

The smells of the fire still hung over Up and Down Farm. When her mother dropped Lucy at the office, a bulldozer was leveling the ground where the North Wing had been. Lucy's hand went to her hip pocket. The day before, in the tack-room ruins, she'd picked up a piece of metal from a bridle. She'd shined it up and it was in her pocket to remind her of how things were before.

Sally ran out of the office. "Lucy. Guess what! You're going to show Whistle on Sunday! Isn't that great?"

"Fantastic!"

"You're supposed to ride Peanuts today and Whistle for the rest of the week."

This day was a roller coaster, Lucy thought. Bad news, then good. Just then a broad-shouldered, dark-haired guy walked out of the stable annex, leading Moonrock to the paddock. Here was another drop on the coaster. She had known that Mr. Kendrick would hire a new groom. But seeing him there was different; the fantasy of bringing Tom back was over.

Chapter Eleven

There was a round of applause as Lucy took the last jump. The stable kids, as always, were whooping it up for one of their own, but out of the corner of her eye Lucy saw Mrs. Hodgson clapping too. Lucy patted Whistle's neck and trotted from the ring.

It had been quite a struggle for Up and Down riders to get to a show nine days after the fire, but you wouldn't know it. The ribbons were piling up.

Debby rushed to Lucy at the outgate. "You've got it so far. That was beautiful!"

"Thanks. It felt good."

Mr. Kendrick joined them. "Let Allistair clean up Whistle for Ladies' Hunter. You can pick up your ribbon on foot."

Lucy and Debby exchanged a look. It was a large class, maybe thirty-six kids. Yet Mr. Kendrick was saying Lucy would be pinned for sure.

Allistair, the new groom, held Whistle's bridle as Lucy swung off the horse. "I'll bring her to you at the outside course. You're going third."

"You've got to admit he's good," Debby said as Allistair walked off with the mare.

"Yeah. Come on, let's see the rest of the class."

The August heat steamed through Lucy's jacket as she stood at the rail. The temperature had made a tough show tougher. The number of horses still recovering from the fire and the shortage of tack had meant lots of switching and sharing.

"It's great for Mr. Kendrick that we're doing so well," Debby said happily. "Do you think it's because we didn't expect anything much?"

"You might be right. Everyone just relaxed," Lucy said. That's everyone but me, she thought. Her father had left the night before. And even though things were a mess at home, she had to keep thinking of a way to find the owner of Box 171. But she was trying to put the tension to work. Mr. Kendrick had explained that once. "Focus the tension on the job at hand. Then it will help you instead of getting in the way."

The last rider left the ring; the judge and the ring steward followed. When the steward returned he carried a silver trophy and colored ribbons. There was something reassuring about the predictable order of the colors: always the same blue, red, yellow, white, pink, and green.

The loudspeaker crackled and the announcer began: "We have the results of class twenty-two. First, number forty-two, Lucy Hill. Second, number ten . . ."

Lucy trotted into the ring on foot ahead of the other winners on horseback. Only one more "first" and good-bye Limit. She'd be an Open rider at last. Too bad Whistle couldn't have worn the blue ribbon out of the ring. The mare had made the winning easy.

Mr. Kendrick was at the outgate. "You earned it, Lucinda," he said quietly.

"Nice work, honey. You looked beautiful on that gray horse."

"Mom! When did you get here? I thought you weren't coming."

"I changed my mind," Mrs. Hill said. As Mr. Kendrick walked off, she added, "You've had a difficult week and I'm proud of the way you've kept yourself steady. I was proud of you just now too."

Lucy blinked in surprise. Her mother rarely gave her compliments.

"Thanks, Mom. Will you walk me to the outside course? I'm showing Silver Whistle over there in a Hunter class. This time they judge the horse, not the rider. But it's up to me to make her look good."

As they crossed the show grounds, Lucy reminded herself: focus the tension. Forget about Mom and Dad and the stable and the unidentified owner of Box 171! Lucy realized that her mother was struggling to keep up and she made herself walk more slowly. She took a deep breath and felt herself begin to calm down. To her surprise it was really a help to have her mother there.

The lampshade on Lucy's night table was reserved for blue ribbons only. She hooked the new rosette over the edge. Six on the flat, five over fences. One still missing. But right now a missing name seemed even more important.

"Debby, I have to talk to you," Lucy said into the upstairs phone minutes later.

"What's up?"

"I need your help."

"How?"

"To collect names on a petition in front of the post office tomorrow."

"You must be kidding. You're going to miss riding for *that?*"

"Tomorrow's Monday, silly. The stable's closed."

"I didn't know you were into any causes. What kind of a petition?"

"To save endangered wildlife. We both believe in that. But really it will just be an excuse to sit outside the post office from the time it opens until it closes."

"Some people are very serious about these issues. I don't think we should be making fun of them."

"Tell you what. We'll send in the petitions to the right organization."

"You're too much." Debby laughed. "Why in front of the post office?"

"I'll explain tomorrow. Mom's got an old bridge table we can use. Do you have some folding chairs?"

"I think so. Am I supposed to follow you blindly?"

"Yes!"

"Okay. How about lunch? I'll get Tina to pack some."

"Lunch with brownies?"

"What else! It might be fun. The post office opens at eight thirty. Bryan and I will pick you up at a quarter after eight. We better get some sleep."

No wonder Debby was her best friend. Lucy jumped onto her bed so hard that the box spring thudded against the frame. She smoothed the ends of her new blue ribbon and turned out the light.

*   *   *

"Who said this was going to be fun?" Lucy said as she returned to the card table after a dash around the mailboxes.

The same routine had been going on all morning. The card table was positioned so that Lucy and Debby could see into the post office. If a person walked through the glass doors and kept on straight ahead, there was no need to get up. If a person walked through the glass doors and turned left to the mailboxes, Debby or Lucy had to run to see which box they stopped at.

"Now!" At Lucy's nudge Debby raced up the steps.

"Is your friend all right?" A gray-haired woman in pink sneakers was standing in front of the table.

"Yes . . . she . . . isn't this a great stuffed panda? I've had it since I was little. We thought it would attract attention." Lucy straightened up the toy animal.

"I suppose. What do you want me to sign?"

"Here's our petition." Lucy had worked out the language from a pamphlet she'd found in Eric's room.

"Hm . . ." the woman mumbled. ". . . urge protection of habitats . . . prevent exploitation by hunters and fishermen. . . . Hm . . ." She looked at Lucy sternly. "Whooping cranes are an endangered species. I don't see them mentioned here. And how about hawksbill sea-turtles?"

Lucy tried not to burst out laughing at the funny-sounding names and the woman's fussy manner. A man in a striped polo shirt walked up the post office steps. When he continued straight ahead, Lucy answered, "There are over a thousand endangered species. We thought whales, sea otters, and condors were enough examples."

"Have you any pamphlets to distribute?"

"There's only this one left, but you're welcome to look at it here."

Debby slid into her seat and moved her head from side to side.

"I don't think you girls are serious enough about what you're doing," the woman said suddenly. She walked off shaking her head with disapproval.

"She should know," Lucy laughed.

"When do we eat?" Debby said.

"It won't look good to eat out here."

"What choice do we have?"

"Hello, Lucy, Debby. How come you're not at the stable?" Mrs. Rose, Joey's mother, was patting the stuffed panda.

"It's Monday," Lucy said, smiling a greeting. "How's Joey? Shouldn't he be out of the hospital soon? It's over two weeks already."

"He's getting along. There were internal injuries, you know, so we've had some problems . But he'll be fine."

"Say hello to him for us," Lucy said.

"Right!" Debby added.

"I certainly will. I'll sign your petition too."

"She's neat," Debby said, as Mrs. Rose walked off.

"Oops, it's my turn!" Lucy leapt to her feet and hurried through the glass doors after a woman in green slacks. To the left, row after row of mailboxes were arranged in a large square island in the center of the room. Lucy walked along the bottom aisle and turned right. The woman in green was collecting her mail a short distance ahead. So much for that. At the top of the square Lucy picked out Box 171. To make it easier to locate she'd put a small red sticker on the box above.

As Lucy turned right a final time and started for the door, she stopped short. A bald, heavyset man was charging into the room and he looked very familiar.

Lucy held absolutely still. She listened to his footsteps as they crossed the bottom aisle and turned right. He moved up the next aisle. He turned right again. Now he was at the top of the square. He stopped.

Concealing her excitement, Lucy strolled back the way she'd come. The man was pulling envelopes out of Box 171. It was, she realized, the man she'd seen leave Mr. Kendrick's apartment a few months ago. So *he* owned the fields!

When she reached the far aisle, Lucy leaned against the wall and collected her thoughts. She'd half-expected to see Bolton. She had thought of *him* as Mr. Kendrick's number-one enemy.

When Lucy thought the coast was clear, she hurried back to Debby. There were two little kids at the table talking about whales, but Debby got rid of them at Lucy's signal.

"Well, we can have lunch anytime we want," Lucy said.

"You're kidding. That man who just walked down the steps? I don't believe it."

"Why not? He's a land developer who's on the Town Council. Sally told me about him."

Debby wasn't listening. "You're sure it was Box 171 he went to?"

"I'm sure. What's the problem?"

"He drove off in a blue Oldsmobile Cutlass."

"So? That's his car. I've seen him in it."

"He wasn't driving, Lucy. That's the point. Jim, the handyman, was driving the car."

Like everyone in Westlake, Lucy was very familiar with the two-story white building, a block from the village green, where the weekly newspaper was published. She'd often looked through the large downstairs window at the reporters typing away at their stories. But it was different to be inside the building, especially in the formal second-floor office of the editor and publisher. Lucy could hardly believe she'd had the courage to phone Henny. The idea had popped into her head after Debby dropped her at home, and Henny had said to come right over.

"What can I do for you, Lucy?" Behind her beautiful mahogany desk Henny was almost walled in by books and papers. She fixed Lucy with a direct stare.

"Uh—thanks for seeing me, Mrs. Gibney. I know how busy you are."

"I thought you'd be bringing me a story."

"You did!"

"Just a hunch. But it's hunches that make good newspapermen—excuse me, newspaperpersons."

"Well, I might be on the track of a story. I've been thinking a lot about everything that's happened at Up and Down Farm, and I've got some ideas. But I need help. I can't go any farther myself."

"Don't the police suspect the groom, Tom Roberts?"

"Yes, but you see, I got to know him, and . . . anyway, I don't think what's happened has to do with vandalism or 'the acts of someone disturbed,' as the police have been saying. I think a person with something special to gain is at work. Someone who wants to force Mr. Kendrick to sell Up and Down Farm."

Henny leaned back in her chair. One hand crept up to her beads. "My goodness, Lucy. That's quite a charge."

"I know. That's why I came to *you*. I didn't want to go to Mr. Kendrick without proof."

"Do you have a suspect of your own?"

"I think so. I feel as though—as though I'm holding a zipper that's stuck. I thought you could help me close it."

"That's a nice image. Are the Hills going to have still another writer in the family?"

"I don't think so."

"Certainly not unless you can be more definite. Formulate your thoughts and state them."

"Okay, I'll start with Mr. Rupert. I know he owns the fields on either side of Up and Down Farm, and—"

"What makes you think that?" Henny said sharply. "My information is different."

"I checked at Town Hall."

"Did you!"

"The woman there told me that the two parcels were sold to the Wilmont Development Corporation five months ago. Then Debby and I staked out their post office box."

Henny hitched her chair closer to the desk and leaned forward. "The fact that someone picked up the mail doesn't mean that they own the company, Lucy. But you happen to be correct. Wilmont Development *is* Rupert's company. I didn't know that he'd bought the fields, but he developed the property across the Main Road from Kendrick too."

That was interesting news. Mr. Rupert must be planning to build more houses. The squeeze on Mr. Kendrick was from *three* sides!

"What brought you to the Hall of Records, Lucy? Would you like a cold drink? Make yourself comfortable. I'm interested in what you have to say."

"I'm fine, thanks, Miss Gibney." Lucy tried to relax against the high-backed chair, but her hands still gripped the arms. "I've been working on this for weeks. At first I thought the Hodgsons were to blame, trying to take business away from Mr. Kendrick. I know it sounds awful, but the rumors started me off, and . . . anyway, I was wrong.

"Then I thought of Mr. Bolton. He wants Mr. Kendrick to lose the election so the shopping mall will pass. He'd also like the contract to build it. He could have paid someone to help him."

"I see—like Tom."

"No. I don't think Tom's part of this at all. And I'm not so sure about Mr. Bolton anymore, either."

"Now you think it's Donald Rupert."

Lucy shifted uncomfortably under Henny's intense stare. She wasn't going to fold, *now*. "I think it's Donald Rupert plus Jim, the handyman. Mr. Rupert wants to get Mr. Kendrick off the Town Council, too, but I'm convinced his main goal is to buy the farm. I think he wants to put together another big tract of land to build on and Mr. Kendrick's right in the middle—"

"And how do you tie Jim to Rupert?"

"For one thing, the problems at the stable started just about the time he came. And today, we *saw* him with Mr. Rupert. Jim was chauffeuring Mr. Rupert around town!"

"Lucy, you're going too fast. You must learn to follow a story step by step and check out the evidence as you go."

"Don't I have evidence, Miss Gibney?"

"Circumstantial evidence, at best, and not very solid. You're right that Jim works for Mr. Rupert. He's a carpenter and Donald Rupert puts up houses. Jim moonlights for extra money."

How could she have missed such a simple connection? But she wasn't letting go of Jim yet!

"Miss Gibney, you said you had faith in hunches. Well, I've got a hunch that might give us a lot of answers. The trouble is I can't follow it up without help. I don't have a driver's license." She swallowed hard. "If you'd be willing to drive me somewhere tomorrow afternoon . . ."

"Aren't you the clever one. I'm 'hoist by my own petard.' "

Lucy didn't have the faintest idea what that meant. But she could tell from the expression on Henny's face that her answer was going to be yes.

Chapter Twelve

As Lucy and Henny walked up to the small wooden house the next afternoon, Mrs. Walker opened the door slightly and poked her head out. "It's Miss Gibney and Lucy Hill." She threw the door wide open. "Come in. We've been so excited since you called."

Henny, decked out in lilac and blue for tea, stepped into the house. Lucy admired the eccentric woman more than ever. Driving out in the antique car, Henny had never once asked about the purpose of this visit. She'd made it clear that Lucy was to carry the ball.

"Come in, come in. Mr. Walker's in here." Lucy tried not to stare. Mrs. Walker was not even five feet tall, and all of the furniture seemed unusually small. Lucy felt as though a tiny aged doll was leading them into a dollhouse.

In the front room Nick unfolded himself out of an oversized arm chair, the one piece of furniture scaled to his size.

"Why, Miss Gibney, what a pleasure to see you. And it's Lucy . . . the Hill girl." He turned to Mrs. Walker. "Why didn't you say so?"

"I did. I did. Lucy Hill is what I said."

"Well, never mind." His eyes were merry. "After all these years am I going to make the newspaper, Miss Gibney?"

"That depends," Henny said heartily. "What have you been up to?"

"Mending my old bones, that's what."

"Sit down, please do sit down." Mrs Walker's hands fluttered toward an old couch on which patches of fabric had been neatly tacked. "I've prepared some tea and cookies. The kind I make for our two great-grandchildren." Her eyes twinkled. "Nick made them their own Up and Down Farm, you know." She waved to a rectangular mound in the corner, covered with a clean sheet.

"Will you show it to us?" Lucy asked.

"After a bit." Nick looked at Lucy affectionately. "You know, Miss Gibney, all those years on roofs and ladders, I did a lot of looking *down* on these young ones growing up." He chuckled at his joke. "I seen them tossed into the saddle with stirrups in the very first hole. The next thing they're out in the fields raising the fences behind Kendrick's back."

"I'm going for the tea, Nick. Don't talk the guests to death."

"Nick," Lucy said, "I know you were hurt badly when you fell. You seem just great now."

"All of us Walkers are healers. Otherwise we couldn't keep on being Walkers. Get it?" He chuckled. "I'm a little bit stiff in a lot of places. But I was lucky. It could have been worse."

"How come, Nick? Why do you say that?"

"Let me tell you about that accident," Nick said, with some bitterness in his voice.

Just then Mrs. Walker returned with tea and a plate of oatmeal cookies. "Nick," she said quickly, "I'm sure the company would rather look at your miniature stable than hear that old story."

For a moment Nick seemed uncertain. Then he walked across the room and whisked the sheet from a large model stable. Lucy located a tack room, a feed bin, and a hayloft. Tiny bridles hung on pegs next to saddles, a pitchfork stood up in a bale of hay.

"Remarkable," Henny said.

"It's unbelievable!" Lucy gasped.

Mrs. Walker said proudly, "He adds things all the time."

"You see, my old fingers can still work fine." Nick brought over a tiny tack-trunk with working hinges. "Edna's shy. She won't tell you she made this little pair of chaps to go inside."

Lucy marveled at more details of the stable, but she was impatient to ask her questions.

At last Nick replaced the sheet. "That fire was a terrible thing," he said, returning to his chair. "Wish I could fix up the big barn as easy as this one."

Lucy said quickly, "You'd be over there helping if you hadn't been hurt. You were starting to tell me how you fell."

"It's not important," Mrs. Walker interrupted. "Nick was going to retire in three months any-way—when he turned seventy-five."

Nick looked at his wife. "Now, Edna, never you mind. This is my chance to talk."

"It *is* important, Mrs. Walker, please."

"Nick," Henny said, "we'd like to hear what you have to say."

"Was there something wrong with the ladder?"
Lucy prompted.

"You know the metal crosspiece attached to each
side of a stepladder? Well, if one of them crosspieces
comes loose, the ladder's going to walk away. It's
going to splay open and fall over sideways."

"How would a crosspiece come loose?"

"If a nut came off one of the bolts."

"But you check the nuts."

"Sure thing. Screw them down as tight as they go.
That ladder should have been safe."

"A tight nut doesn't unscrew itself," Henrietta
said. "Did you tell John that you thought someone
had tampered with the ladder?"

"No, Miss Gibney. By the time I came back to myself, there didn't seem much point."

"It's a hard thing to expect anyone to believe,"
Mrs. Walker said. "Who at the stable would do such
a thing?"

"Nick, when you started up the ladder, couldn't
you feel that something was wrong?"

"No, the bolt was still in place, Lucy. But without
the nut, it worked loose. Someone tampered with
that ladder. I know they did."

The elderly man's face was flushed and he was
breathing fast. Mrs. Walker stood up and started to
clear the tea things away.

"Just one more question," Lucy said in a rush. "You
know the wooden bridge over the creek?"

"The trail bridge? Sure," Nick answered.
"Checked them boards couple of times a year."

"One of the newest boards broke a few months

ago. It looked as if there was dry rot toward the bottom."

"Not on *that* bridge, there wasn't!" Nick banged the table. "I checked every board twice, at the lumberyard and at the bridge."

"Lucy, Nick has been very helpful, don't you think?" Henrietta got to her feet. "It's been a delightful visit, Mr. and Mrs. Walker. And informative too. Now we really must go."

A few minutes later Henny cranked up the old car as Lucy watched from the high, uncomfortable seat. Despite the hard surface Lucy felt like bouncing up and down with excitement. Now if only Henny, too, had been convinced by Nick's story.

Henny climbed into the car and they started down the road. "Well, it was a good hunch," she said at last.

"You really think so?"

"I just said so."

"I mean, you agree that Nick's accident was rigged?"

"Nick's sure that it was." Henny thought a moment. "Yes. He convinced me."

"Then Jim must have caused the accident so he could apply for the job himself?"

"There was no certainty that Kendrick would hire Jim. We've other carpenters in Westlake."

"But Mr. Kendrick knew Jim already. He worked with Mrs. Kendrick at school. It was a reasonable chance."

"How could Jim get to the ladder?"

"Nick often left a ladder against the barn if the weather was good. Jim could have come around at night."

"All right," Henny said. "Let's assume that Nick's accident was arranged so that Jim could become his replacement. Can we accept that Jim was responsible for all the trouble that followed? Why wasn't anyone suspicious? He must have been around the stable at odd hours."

"So was Nick, when he worked there. No one would have thought anything of it. Tom's the only one who might have seen something unusual, and he wouldn't have said."

"Was Jim at the stable when the accident took place at the bridge?"

Lucy thought a moment. "Yes. He'd been there a few days."

Henny took her eyes off the road and looked at Lucy squarely. "You realize that we have not one bit of hard proof. Not about Jim, not about a conspiracy . . ." She turned back to the road. "Let's just think quietly."

Lucy glanced over at Henny gratefully. Her back was as straight as though in a brace, and the ribbons from her hat hung down between her shoulders. One hand was playing with her beads. Lucy began to think.

"Have you any ideas, Lucy?" Henny asked, as they reached the Westlake line.

"I've an idea, Miss Gibney, but it depends on you."

"Yes?"

"We've got to get Jim to save his own skin by testifying against Rupert. We've got to scare him into confessing, somehow."

"I'm formidable, Lucy, but I can't put anyone through the third degree."

"Well, maybe we could write some kind of a story in the paper. . . ."

"What kind of a story?"

Lucy took a deep breath and plunged on. "I was thinking that Joey Rose is still in the hospital. If Jim thought Joey was dying, or even that he . . . or . . . or . . . I mean, if Jim thought he was in more trouble than he's expected—"

"Lucy Hill, are you suggesting that I print a false story? Are you impugning the journalistic ethics of the *Westlaker?*"

Lucy stiffened. "I'm sorry. It was just an idea."

"Well, it can't be done," Henny said flatly. "But you've made me think. I'll have to consult John Kendrick, and I'll telephone you first thing in the morning."

"I hope he won't be mad at me."

"We'll talk about it in the morning." Henny's tone made clear that the subject was closed.

"I really appreciate this ride out to Nick's, Miss Gibney," Lucy said after a while.

"You're welcome, Lucy; it was very worthwhile. Where do you want me to take you, to your house or to the stable?"

"Home, I think."

"You must learn to be more definite. And—I want a promise, Lucy. You're not to speak to anyone about this until I give you permission. Understood? Not your friends, not your parents."

"I promise, Miss Gibney."

"Why don't you call me Henny?"

Chapter Thirteen

Lucy had started her weekly pool chores at eight o'clock to be ready for whatever Henny had in mind. As she cleaned out the filters, she listened for the phone on the porch. What kind of a plan had Henny thought up? Was Mr. Kendrick willing to go along? He had been furious when she'd acted on her own at the fire. Was he angry now? Maybe her efforts to solve the mystery seemed out of bounds too.

Lucy rushed for the phone at the first ring.

"Hello?" she heard her mother say.

"Hello, Marion. Henrietta Gibney here. Is that darling daughter of yours at hand?"

"I've got it, Mom," Lucy said quickly. She listened for the click of her mother's receiver. "Hi, Miss Gibney."

"Are you there, Lucy Hill?"

"Certainly, Miss Gib—Henny."

"I hope so, because John Kendrick and I are counting on you to see this caper through."

Whew! He couldn't be *too* angry.

"Fantastic, Henny. What do I do? When do I do it?"

"Now, don't let excitement 'blow you away,' as you

kids say. Come to my office at three thirty tomorrow. Can you do that?"

"Of course."

"Can you ride over here on your bike? Then no questions will be raised."

"Easy. I'll bike from the stable."

"Good. The *Westlaker* comes out tomorrow, remember? I'll have something to show you."

Lucy was startled. It certainly sounded as though she'd bought the idea of the fake story. What had happened to the "journalistic ethics"?

"I can't wait. See you tomorrow."

"By the way, Lucy, John Kendrick had something interesting to tell me. Over the last five months Rupert has tried to buy the farm, not once but several times—"

"Then it all makes sense. Each time Mr. Kendrick said no, Rupert increased the pressure."

"Exactly. Tomorrow then, at three thirty."

"Right. And thanks, Henny. Thanks for taking me seriously."

Henny's loud cackle jumped through the phone. "You're a very serious girl, don't you know?"

On Thursday morning the hot sun steamed through layers of haze. Lucy's damp shirt clung to her skin as she came up to the barn from her lesson. Mr. Kendrick had greeted her with a pat on the back, but hadn't mentioned Henny's call. She looked at her watch. Three more hours to wait.

Debby was already in the stable yard and they walked together, cooling out their horses.

"It's a shame you have to give her up," Debby said,

admiring Whistle from nose to tail. "You looked so good at Stamford. Do you know when Mrs. Kelly's coming back?"

"The mare turns into Peanut Butter at midnight on Monday."

They sponged the horses and were taking them to the barn when Lucy caught sight of a tall, thin figure down at the stable sign on the Main Road. As he turned into the drive a large knapsack bounced between his shoulders with each loping stride.

Lucy's mouth fell open. She wanted to drop Whistle's lead shank and race down the drive, but she forced herself to take the mare to her stall. She was really glad to see Tom, but what would happen to him now? Why had he come back? Was he locked in silence again? If he was talking, what would he say?

When Lucy rushed back outside, Tom was at the paddock talking to Moonrock. She hurried toward him.

"Tom?" she called. "Tom!"

The boy paid no attention even when Lucy reached his side. She tried to make out the words he was murmuring. He was asking Moonrock about the horses and the fire.

"Tom, all the horses are okay, but you shouldn't be here. The police are after you."

Tom turned to her abruptly. *"All* the horses?" His eyes came alive.

"Yes, all! But no thanks to you. What happened the night of the fire? Why did you cut out? Why did you wreck everything for yourself here?"

Tom started to shiver. "My aunt died, the one I talked about." He looked Lucy straight in the eye.

"She left me some cash. That lawyer found my address in her drawer. Once that lawyer finds me, my old man is next."

"Tom, don't you remember? I handed you that lawyer's letter myself. It was three weeks before you left!"

"Didn't know what to do at first." Tom's eyes stayed on her face. "Couldn't think about nothing for a long time. Then Joey got hurt and the police came around."

"Why are you afraid to be found? Because you're under eighteen?"

Tom hung his head. "Altogether, it was time to go. I hitched to Pennsylvania. Got me a job in a barn down there."

"Then how come you're here *now?*"

"This man came to show Mr. Gunther a horse. He said somebody torched Kendrick's barn. I quit my job and hitched back."

"Tom, you don't understand. The police think it's *you* who started the fire."

Tom closed his eyes and kept on talking as though he'd memorized a speech. "I'm not going to run anymore, whatever happens. Mr. Kendrick, he's the most decent man I ever knew. He'll hear me out."

Lucy felt the way she did when she flew to her grandparents in California and the plane hit an air pocket. What could Tom expect from Mr. Kendrick after deserting without a word? And what about the police?

Suddenly Lucy remembered that everything had changed. Her detective work might clear Tom before long.

"You shouldn't have run off, Tom."

"Yeah. If I was here, I'd have caught the creep with the match."

"Not just that. It may not be so easy to come back Mr. Kendrick's hired another groom."

Tom's face tightened. "Well, I can cut out again if I have to."

Lucy was aware of someone behind her. Mr. Kendrick put a hand on her shoulder. "All right, Lucy," he said firmly. "I'll take over now."

After Tom showed up, it was even harder to wait for three thirty. Now Henny's plan was critical for him too.

"Come in, come in," Henny called when, at last, Lucy knocked on her office door.

The day's edition of the *Westlaker* lay open on the desk. Even upside down Lucy could easily read the headline: "Stable Accident Proves Fatal."

"But, Henny, you said you couldn't!" Lucy blurted out.

Henny lifted another newspaper from under the first. "Here's this week's paper, Lucy. I said we couldn't print a false *story*. I said nothing about a false *copy!*" Henny's eyes sparkled. "I set the type myself."

"That's fantastic!" Lucy began to read the story:

Joey Rose, the ten-year-old boy injured in a riding accident several weeks ago, died this morning at Fairmont Hospital. The police now maintain that the accident was caused by a manmade hole, camouflaged on the far side of the jump.

Police Chief Yaffe told this reporter, "We have a new witness who claims to have seen a tall, brown-haired man, about thirty-five-years-old in the vicinity of the jump course with a shovel the night before the accident. We now suspect that the man dug the hole in question." Chief Yaffe emphasized that Joey's death raises this act to the category of murder.

"Wow, Henny!" Lucy said. "That should crack him."

"We'll see. It's your responsibility to put this copy of the paper into Jim's car sometime before he normally leaves the stable. And you mustn't be seen."

"What if Jim has already read a copy of the real paper?"

"That's unlikely, don't you think? We're not on the stands until well after lunch and Jim works all afternoon."

"I guess it doesn't matter. The fake paper in his car will still let him know that someone's wise to him."

"Exactly."

"I wonder what Jim will do? He might just run away."

"That's a chance we'll have to take. John Kendrick thinks Jim will come to him for help. He's known Jim a long time."

Henny handed Lucy the paper. "Now be off with you. I might get a real story out of this for next week's *Westlaker.*"

At five o'clock Lucy positioned herself in the office doorway.

"You're certainly edgy today," Sally said. "Tom

will be okay. I don't see why, but Mr. Kenderick's sheltering him for the night. What if the police find out?"

"Did Mr. Kendrick and Tom leave here together?"

"Yes, but Mr. K. came back. He's in the apartment and doesn't want to be disturbed. I certainly don't understand what's going on around here."

"Don't worry. Mr. Kendrick usually has good reasons for what he does."

Sally shook her head. "For the first time in my life I'm not sure."

Through the screen door Lucy saw Jim walk out of the barn toward his car.

"When's your mother coming to pick you up?" Sally said. "You're making me nervous."

"I'm going to call her any minute." Jim was opening the car door. "I wasn't sure what time I'd be through today."

"What are you talking about?" Sally said. "You didn't have a lesson this afternoon."

Jim started the motor. He must not have noticed the newspaper; she'd left it on the passenger side of the front seat. Maybe he'd seen the folded paper but hadn't opened it up.

Lucy stepped out of the office. The car motor was still running but the T-bird hadn't moved. Through the back window she saw Jim reading the paper. She walked a short way down the drive as though watching for her mother.

All of a sudden the car motor stopped. Jim stepped out of the car and began to walk toward Mr. Kendrick's apartment. The fake newspaper was in his hand.

Lucy took a deep breath and exhaled slowly. So far the plan was working. After all these years she might be able to give something back to Mr. Kendrick and Up and Down Farm for all they'd done for her. It had never seemed possible before.

Lucy hurried back to the office. "I'll be quiet as a mouse," she said, settling down on the wooden bench. If she could hang around for a while she might get a clue to what was happening in the apartment. She read the latest issue of the *Chronicle of the Horse.* She got up and studied the old pictures on the walls of Kendrick horses and riders from three generations. She sat down again, picked up a windbreaker someone had left behind, and looked for the name tape.

"Are you jagged up today! I'm filling out insurance forms and I've got to concentrate. Will you *please* call your mother!"

"Okay, okay." Lucy went to the phone and lifted the receiver. Her body froze at the sound of voices. She listened as long as she dared, then hung up gently. Mr. Kendrick had been talking to the police, arranging to bring Jim to the station.

Chapter Fourteen

"Keep talking! I can't believe you kept all this from your best friend for four whole days."

Debby held a can of neat's-foot oil in one hand. She had been using it to soften a new saddle when Lucy found her in the tack room on Sunday. She fixed her dark eyes on Lucy. "So what happened then?"

"Thursday, after Jim got the fake paper, Henny called me at home to say we'd pulled it off. Jim had confessed to Mr. Kendrick and later to the police. I was busting to tell you, but I wasn't allowed to say a word until the police had Rupert in custody."

"And they nabbed him this morning?"

"Yeah!! Mr. Kendrick invited me to the apartment and gave me the fake newspaper as a souvenir. He said, 'It's yours by rights.' "

"It's hard to believe Jim did all those things," Debby said, starting to work on the saddle again. "He seemed like a pretty nice guy and he was great with the kids."

"He went along with Rupert for the money. Henny says Jim's the kind of person who does things without thinking of the consequences. When Joey was hurt he tried to back out of the deal but Rupert

threatened him into starting the fire. Jim was the unidentified man who phoned in the alarm. He hoped
the firemen would get here before too much damage
was done."

"Wow! We always said he wasn't very bright. Will
Jim get a break for testifying against Rupert?"

"Yes, but he won't get off altogether. He'll do at
least some time in jail."

Lucy leaned against the wooden saddle-rack. Telling Debby the news had picked up her spirits but she
was sagging again. Now that the case was closed,
there was nothing to take her mind off the new de-
velopments at home.

"You should feel terrific," Debby said proudly.
"Joan of Arc at Up and Down Farm."

"Come on, Deb. Don't be stupid."

"You should be triumphant. You look miserable."

"I'm okay." She wasn't ready to tell anyone, even
Debby, about the decisions her parents had made in
the last few days.

"Don't feel badly about sending Jim to jail. He de-
serves it," Debby said. "Nick could have been killed
and Joey too. The horses could all have died in the
fire. The barn could have been totaled—"

"It's not that—"

"Come on, Lucy, we found a place." Paul grabbed
Lucy's hand and began to pull. Carol stood behind
him holding a small box.

Grateful for the interruption, Lucy said to Debby,
"We're going to bury Carol's gerbil."

"Is this a cemetery?" Debby asked.

"It's my favorite place," Carol said solemnly. "I
want Jeremy to stay here."

"Let's go," Lucy said, unaccountably close to tears.

The place the children had chosen for Jeremy's grave was just beyond the outside course. It was exactly the spot where the little girl had darted out of the bushes after her puppy. As the children argued over a hymn that everyone would know, Lucy thought back to the first day she'd suspected a threat to Up and Down Farm. It seemed more like three years than three months.

"How do you know what religion Jeremy was?" Paul asked.

"Same as Carol, silly, he was her gerbil," Virginia said.

"Gerbils are just part of the universe," Paul proclaimed.

"How about 'My Country, 'Tis of Thee?' He was an American gerbil, wasn't he?"

Her Up and Downs were on the plus side of the summer. Now all of them could trot fairly well. And today had been a banner day. The whole class had cantered on the correct lead at one time, *all* of them!

"Make the hole deeper."

"Domino will dig it up if you don't."

There was much giggling until Carol jabbed Paul in the stomach. Then the kids began to sing.

Listening to the odd chorus, Lucy thought how her father often said, "Life writes its own script." She'd never understood quite what he meant, but this summer must be an example. Almost nothing had worked out the way she had planned. Putting an end to the attack on the stable hadn't solved Mr. Kendrick's problems. Even though the jump course and the barn looked better than ever, it would be a long time before people forgot about the rumors and lies and stopped connecting Up and Down Farm with disasters like accidents and fires.

"Let's find a stone to mark the grave."

"Or a stick."

The one person who'd come out ahead was Tom. All the charges had been dismissed and Mr. Kendrick was taking an interest in his problems. And today he was back at the barn.

As for herself, her Dad was going to be in California. And worse still—

"That's that." Carol clapped the dirt off her hands. "Who wants to come to my house for a swim? You come, Lucy!"

"Thanks, Carol, but I have to ride." As the kids rushed off, Lucy said to herself, Right, you have to ride. Keep your mind on that. That's what always works out best.

Lucy strolled back to the barn with Peanut Butter after a rough hour in the heat. As they poked along, she wondered if horses could imagine a drink of water the way she could look forward to a soft drink.

"Hello, Green-eyes."

"Hi, Allistair."

Lucy looked up at the new apartment where Allistair was painting the window trim. Somehow she didn't mind the nickname. He made it sound like her special name instead of a come-on. It was lucky he was so good at painting and carpentry. Mr. Kendrick was going to move him into Jim's spot as handyman and take Tom back as head groom.

As Lucy unsaddled Peanuts in the stable yard, Tom

led Moonrock out of the annex. The big horse was saddled and bridled. They seemed to be headed for the Main Ring.

"How do you figure that?" Lucy asked Liz, who was passing by with Shogun. "Mr. Kendrick never rides in the ring this early in the day."

"And why would he pick a scorcher like this?"

The clatter of hooves on cement turned both girls toward the barn. Mrs. Kelly led Whistle over to the mounting block and swung into the saddle.

"Hello, girls."

"Hi, Mrs. Kelly. Hi, Whistle, baby."

Mrs. Kelly gave the mare's neck a few affectionate slaps. "There's your good friend Lucy, who saved your life. Just put up with me for a while and she'll take you to the shows again next summer!" They moved off toward the trails.

"Lucy! You'll get to show Whistle next summer! Didn't you hear?"

"Who knows where I'll be next summer?"

"What's the matter? What's happened?"

"I'm just crabby. I'm going to give Peanuts a bath."

"Okay, fella. At least one of us is comfortable." Perspiration was running down Lucy's back but Peanuts was clean and dry. She'd rubbed his legs with liniment and wrapped them with bandages. Lucy sent the horse into his stall with a swat on the rump and rubbed her sleeve across her forehead. How could Mr. Kendrick ride in this heat? It didn't make sense.

Suddenly she had the answer. She hurried out of the barn and down the stable drive. She caught her breath as she came close enough to see the horse and rider circling the Main Ring. They were moving at a slow canter, the big horse collected together and the rider tight in the saddle, as though molded in one piece. She came up to the rail and Tom gave her a shy smile as he passed.

Lucy was mesmerized as Tom seemed to put on a riding exhibition especially for her. After a final round of fences he pulled the horse back to a walk and looped around to Lucy.

"You're terrific, Tom. When did you start to ride him?"

"Last night."

As he trotted off again, Lucy looked after him. Now Tom would have a new life, a happy life, working around horses with people who would treat him fairly.

The misery Lucy had been fighting back all day washed over her. At the sound of footsteps she screwed up her face and closed her eyes to stop the tears.

"Dirt in your eyes, Lucinda?" Mr. Kendrick said.

"No—I mean, yes—but it's okay now."

They watched Tom canter a slow circle in front of the jumps. "He looks good, doesn't he?" Mr. Kendrick said.

"Sure does. Will you give him lessons?"

"Whatever he needs. He's got the best pair of hands I've seen." He called to Tom, "There's too much bend in the left elbow." After several moments he said to Lucy, "If he keeps on looking so good I might let him show Moonrock next year."

For a moment Lucy wondered why they would skip the winter shows. Then she remembered that

Tom still wasn't eighteen. As if he'd read her mind, Mr. Kendrick added, "We'll keep him out of sight till he adds a few months."

Once again Lucy screwed up her face. This time the tears leaked past her eyelids. When she opened her eyes, Mr. Kendrick was looking right at her.

"There's more than dirt to this, Lucy. What's it all about?"

Lucy forgot to steady her voice. "There's something I have to tell you. I've been putting it off for the last few days, but it's not going to change."

"I'll be with you after Lucy and I finish talking," Mr. Kendrick shouted to Tom. Then he turned his back to the ring and leaned against the fence. "All right, Lucinda, what is it?"

"Things have been coming apart at our house this summer. With my parents, I mean. My father's going to California and Mom and me . . ." She couldn't say it. Somehow putting it in words gave her no escape.

"You're going to live with your mother?"

"Yes. But not here."

That small muscle on the side of Mr. Kendrick's face moved back and forth. "Well, now. That's a big one. Where will you be going?"

"New York. At least for this winter. It was decided last night for sure. Mom has to go back to work, so we're renting our house. It's supposed to be just until she figures things out . . . maybe just until the summer . . ."

Mr. Kendrick dipped his pipe into his tobacco pouch and filled it slowly. Then he put a match to the bowl. He looked at Lucy with open affection.

"There's been a lot going on these last months. I guess we've both got a few pieces to put together."

"I thought when we uncovered Mr. Rupert's rotten scheme your troubles would be over. But things aren't that simple, are they?"

"No, Lucy, they're not. But time will take care of a lot. And I've made some new plans too. Young people today go in for 'showing' in a big way. I'm going to find a good young trainer who can concentrate on the show circuit. He can polish up my Juniors and bring us home a Maclay from the Garden. Maybe you'll be the one to pick it up, Lucy. I've always said you had talent."

Hadn't he understood? It had been hard enough to say it once. "Mr. Kendrick, that's why I'm so upset. I'm not sure I'll be here to see what happens to Tom or my Up and Downs or to win anything at all." She was too worn out now for tears. Ramming her hands into her pockets, she felt the metal bridle part she'd found in the ashes of the fire. She turned it round and round in her fingers.

"Won't you be able to ride with me some weekends?" Mr. Kendrick said.

"Maybe once in a while. But Mom's picked a school that's really tough and she says I'll have to settle down there. I'll be allowed to ride in the city, but it won't be anything like working here with you!"

Mr. Kendrick drew on his pipe. "Your mother's not selling the house. You'll probably be back, and I'll be here a long time yet. Do you know how this spread came to be called Up and Down Farm?"

"I always thought it had something to do with the beginning riders."

"Most people do. No, the name was Wexford Farms for years—after the part of Ireland where my family lived. Then my grandfather changed the name to match the farm's 'up and down' fortunes."

"That's neat!"

"I might sell the farm someday. There's no son to carry on for me like I did for my father. But first I'll build up the stable better than it ever was. I'll sell it when I'm good and ready and not before."

"You were in a tight spot this summer for sure. But you always acted as though you'd turn it around somehow. I couldn't bear to hear all those lies about you and to see so many bad things happen. I don't know how you could stand it."

"I'm a lot older than you," Mr. Kendrick said with a smile. "There's one thing you want to remember—the more things you stand up to, the stronger you get."

"I'd have been scared about what was coming next." Lucy sighed deeply. "I guess that's what scares me now."

"You were a very little girl when you came here to me. You couldn't even post—like those youngsters that you start out. But now you can take a lot of horse over a four-foot fence as easy as anything. Sometimes that horse does something you don't expect. He refuses. He runs out. But you're a strong-enough rider to handle it. You'll keep on getting stronger until you can handle just about anything."

Lucy felt herself getting very quiet inside as she listened for what Mr. Kendrick would say next. "We can't figure out everything in life," he went on. "We can just get strong enough to hang on."

Tom trotted over to the fence behind them. "Can I take him up? He's had enough."

Mr. Kendrick nodded. Silently, he and Lucy watched Tom and Moonrock start off for the barn.

"That's what *he*'s doing, Lucy. He's hanging on good. And he can thank you for most of it."

Lucy started to answer, but she found she needed to swallow. She looked at Tom and past him to the Indoor Ring, the office, and the barn.

Mr. Kendrick put an arm over her shoulder and they began to walk together. She gripped the piece of metal in her pocket. She was going to hang on to Mr. Kendrick's words just as hard. Her eyes swept over the fields from the line of trees on the west to the woods on the east. The beauty of the land and the happiness she'd known there were overwhelming. Mr. Rupert hadn't been able to take Up and Down Farm away from Mr. Kendrick. No one would be able to take it away from her, either, even if she never saw the sign at the driveway again.